A Soldier's Wish

Tia Marlee

A Novel Choice Press

Book Cover by Sunset Rose Books

Editing by Lia Huntington

Proofreading by Jammom Reads

This book is dedicated to all those who serve in the military and their families. Thank you for your service.

Contents

Prologue   1

1. Heath   7

2. Gabby   13

3. Heath   19

4. Gabby   25

5. Heath   33

6. Gabby   39

7. Heath   45

8. Gabby   51

9. Heath   57

10. Gabby   63

11. Heath   69

12. Gabby   75

13. Heath   83

14. Gabby   89

15. Heath   99

16. Gabby   105

17. Heath   113

18. Gabby   119

19. Heath   125

20. Gabby   131

21. Heath   137

22. Gabby   143

23. Heath   149

Epilogue   155

About the Author   161

Let's Stay In Touch   162

Also By Tia Marlee   163

Prologue

I glance at the clock on the wall. Fifteen minutes, and I'll hear his voice. I do a little dance; the excitement welling up inside me is too much to contain. Heath's been gone for almost nine months, and my heart hasn't beaten properly the whole time.

"Night, Ms. Daisy," I call, tossing my dirty apron into the hamper and grabbing my bag from under the counter.

"You tell that boy we miss him, ya hear," Ms. Daisy says, and winks at me. I think she suspects we're more than friends, but she's never asked, thank goodness. I like keeping our relationship to ourselves for now. Less pressure that way.

"Will do!" I step outside into the humid night air and hit the unlock button on my key fob. I have five minutes to make it home before Heath video calls me.

Having my best friend, my secret boyfriend, in another state has been harder than I imagined. I got so used to spending nearly every day with Heath that having him gone leaves a gaping hole in my life.

I turn into my quiet neighborhood and squeal. Two minutes.

Our video calls are keeping me sane. To see his face, and hear his voice, helps remind me this is temporary. He's not gone forever. He didn't leave me.

I pull the jeep up the long driveway and put it in park. With one minute to spare, I'm pushing through the front door of the small red brick house that was left to me by my Gram. It's older than dirt, and the floors creak, but it's mine. I kick off my non-skid tennis shoes, a requirement of working at the diner, and run to the desk in the corner of the living room. I open the laptop and jiggle the mouse in time to see the notification pop up that Heath is calling.

My heart leaps in my chest. I take a deep breath and click accept.

Heath's face pops up on my screen, and my smile fades at the look on his face. His brows are drawn together, and his lips pulled down at the corners.

"Hi," I say. "Everything okay?"

Heath nods. "Yeah."

"I'm so happy to see you and hear your voice. It feels like it's been forever." I watch as he looks away.

"I'm being deployed." His words rush out like soda from a shaken-up bottle.

My heart sinks in my chest. I figured it would happen eventually, but I didn't think it would be so soon. "Where?"

He shakes his head and looks at me again. "I'm not allowed to say."

"Oh," I whisper. "For how long?"

"A year. Maybe more." He runs his hands through his cropped hair. "I knew it would happen at some point."

"Yeah," I say quietly, unsure how to respond. "Will you still be able to call?"

He shakes his head. "I don't know. I don't think so."

My eyes burn. I pinch my leg to keep from crying and making this harder on him. "Well, I'll write to you. Every day."

He gives me a smile that doesn't quite reach his eyes. "Thanks, you don't have to do that, though."

"I want to. It's what girlfriends do, isn't it?" I ask, watching as he flinches at my words.

"You know I love you," he starts.

I smile. "I love you, too!" I interrupt. I wonder why he's so nervous. *Wait, is he going to propose?*

"I've been thinking," he says, running his hands over his short-cropped hair.

I take a breath and do my best to stay still. I want him to get the words out so I can scream yes already! "About what?" I say as evenly as possible.

"Us," he says. Hearing that, my heart does a loop in my chest.

"Me too," I say, crossing my fingers in my lap.

"I don't think it's fair to ask you to wait for me."

I don't understand how that's a lead-in to a proposal. "Okay . . ."

"I love you so much, and I'd love to marry you someday. It's just, we're so young—*you're* so young—and the life of a soldier's wife isn't easy."

My heart sinks. Tears prick the back of my eyes. "I . . . what?"

"If we got married and started a family now, you'd be stuck at home with babies, all alone. I'd be gone too much to be a real husband and father. I'm sorry, but I can't ask that of you. It's too much. You deserve more."

I deserve . . . "Heath, we knew this would be hard. I'm okay with hard," I say, desperation making my voice get higher with every word.

He shakes his head. "I can't do that to you. I'm sorry. I'll be home for good in a few years. If you haven't found someone else by then, we can see how we feel."

"Heath, I love you. With my whole heart. That's not going to change." I feel my heart breaking into pieces.

He smiles sadly. "That's just it," he says. "Feelings change all the time. I love you too much to ask you to wait for me. To be on your own, waiting for a call. Relationships are hard when two people are in the same city. They're nearly impossible with so much distance and uncertainty. I can't do it."

Feelings change? Have his feelings changed? "I see," I squeak out. I thought he would be the one that finally chooses me, no matter what. To be there through thick and thin.

I wipe a stray tear from my face. I will not break down.

"Hey, don't cry," he says. His voice is low, soothing. "It hurts me too, but knowing you're happy is what's most important to me. And I don't want to lose you. I still want you to write to me," he continues. "I want to hear about your dates and all the fun things you're doing. You deserve to enjoy these years. Please say we can still be friends."

We're both quiet for a bit. He's watching me and waiting. I can't bring myself to look him in the eye for a minute. Then I nod. "Of course we're friends." I close my eyes and take a deep breath before opening them again.

"Are you okay?" he asks, his eyes glossy.

The tears start to fall, and there's nothing I can do to stop them. "Yes. This was just unexpected. I'll still write. It's fine." My heart is barely beating, my face burns with embarrassment and shame. I'm not worth waiting for. I should have seen it coming. My dad left, then my mom. Gram didn't choose to leave, but she's still gone. I've been so careful to only let people in who I know will stick around, but now I find out I'm not worth the wait to Heath after all.

"I have one more thing I wanted to tell you," Heath says. "I have a friend here who . . ." Heath turns and looks over his shoulder.

There's a ruckus in the background and I see some guys he's stationed with saunter into the room.

"Hey, Heath, you telling your baby momma you won't be there for delivery?" someone calls out.

My brain stutters. *Baby momma?* "Heath, what is he talking about?"

Heath's face is red, his eyes huge. "It's not what you think," he blurts.

"Heath, did you get someone pregnant?" My hands are shaking. Is this why he can't ask me to wait?

"It's not that simple," he says, waving for the guys to stop talking. They are still laughing and telling jokes in the background.

"OOOHHHHHH, it's not baby momma! It's back-home sweetheart!" one guy says, stooping in front of the camera. "I take it you didn't know Heath knocked up one of the other privates?" He shakes his head and tsks. "Heath, my man, you're in trouble now."

"Gabby, please. Just listen," Heath pleads.

"I *have* been listening. I've been listening to you break my heart for the last ten minutes, Heath. Why not just tell me the truth? That's what friends do, right? They tell each other the truth? You're not breaking up with me for my sake . . . you've just already moved on!" I suck in air. "Why not just tell me you found someone better?" I laugh, a shrill sound, even to my own ears.

Heath shakes his head, but I keep talking. Now it's time *he* listens. "You expect me to write to you while you're starting your own new little family? I don't think so."

He motions to the guys to be quiet. "Please," he says.

"Goodbye, Heath." I hit the *end call* button before he can speak again.

Sobs wrack my body. So much for my fairytale ending. Thank goodness we never told anyone we were more than friends. I don't think I could stand the sympathy right now. *Poor little Gabby. No one wants to stick around for her.* No, what they don't know can't hurt me. Right?

I stumble into the bedroom and remove my uniform, tossing it into the hamper. I pull on an oversized shirt Heath left for me to sleep in, fall into my unmade bed and let the tears come.

CHAPTER ONE

Heath

I walk through the door to the apartment I share with my buddies Beckett and James, and grin. I've officially been discharged from the Army. What a surreal feeling. I set my stuff down on the counter and kick off my shoes.

"It's official?" James asks, grabbing the remote and turning down the TV.

"Yep, I'm out." I plop down in the worn recliner and lean back. "The Army no longer owns me." Time to go home. It's been six years since I've been back home. Unless you count the few days I spent there between Christmas and New Year's last year—which I don't. I spent the entire time hiding from anyone I knew.

Sure, I've taken leave, but I couldn't face going back home and seeing her. Not since I'd gone and broken her heart, and mine. Hence the hiding. So anytime I had leave, I did what any red-blooded man would do. I flew my momma anywhere she wanted to go and joined her on the vacations.

"Are you ready to go back home?" James asks, as if he can sense the mood I'm in. If anyone understood being away from their girl, it was James. Except his story will end with a happily ever after, and mine . . . well, it just ended.

I nod. "Yeah, my mom needs me. It's been too long." I was deployed again, this time in South Korea, when she discovered the cancer. I wanted to leave then, but she encouraged me to stay and finish out my enlistment term. Not that they'd have let me leave early, anyway. I rub my hand across the ache in my chest. I should have been there from the start. Going home last year was the only thing that has kept me going until now. Mom insisted she was fine, and I chose to believe her. Though I'm certain "fine" was far from the truth.

"I'm sure she'll be glad to have you home for good," James says, reaching for the remote to rewind the last play of the football game. "The golden boy in all his glory."

I shake my head. "Are *you* ready to go back home?"

James grins. "You bet. The first thing I'm going to do is get on one knee and propose to Janice." He pulls out his phone and tosses it to me. "Check out the screen saver. She sent me a new picture." His girlfriend, a cute, dark-skinned girl with naturally curly hair and a gorgeous smile poses for the photo. "I can't wait."

I push down the envy that swirls in my stomach like sour acid, and force a smile. "Congratulations. I'm sure she'll say yes."

He smiles and looks down at the phone when I hand it back. "My parents have been working with hers to throw me a welcome home party. What Janice doesn't know is that it will be our engagement party, too."

"You popping the question as soon as you get off the plane, or what?" Beckett asks, coming down the hall from his room.

"First chance I get," James replies.

"Well, I'm not telling anyone I'm coming home," Beckett announces. "I'm surprising my folks at church on a Sunday. Haven't you seen those videos of families being reunited? I'll be viral on YouTube or TikTok, or whatever is trending these days." He laughs and rubs his hands together like he's plotting something big.

James raises an eyebrow and smirks. "I'm surprised your antics haven't made you YouTube famous before now."

He's not wrong. Of the three of us, Beckett is the most adventurous.

"Yeah, well, I can't help that the two of you are sticks-in-the-mud." He points at James and then me. "If you guys hadn't been so caught up on your girls back home, you'd have had more time for fun."

I shake my head. "Nah, it's just not my scene."

"Yeah, that and you had the whole Army convinced you were the one who got Olivia pregnant."

I shake my head. Somehow, the three of us have been stationed in the same place since basic training. We haven't been moved as much as some of our fellow soldiers, and for that I'm grateful. Except, that also means these two knuckleheads know all my business.

"Hardy har har," I say, standing from the recliner and rolling my head back to release some of the tension I've been storing there since our last deployment. "I didn't tell anyone I got her pregnant. People made assumptions, and I didn't correct them."

"Seriously," James says, eyeing me. "I'm still surprised you're planning to head back home. I figured you'd stick around Kentucky and stay close to Zade. That kid may not be yours, but he sure has you wrapped around his finger."

I chuckle as I make my way into the small kitchen area and grab a bottle of water from the fridge. "Olivia and Zade are in a good place with Dominic now. Besides, we can do video chats, and I can visit sometimes." I shrug. "It's what uncles do."

"So, it has nothing to do with your hometown sweetheart?" Beckett asks, shooting me a knowing look.

I shake my head. "Nope. You know she ghosted me." I swallow a gulp of water. "I'm going home for my mom. Maybe I'll stay, maybe I won't. We'll see."

The guys nod at the mention of my mom.

"When do you leave?" James asks, throwing the remote on the couch and turning his attention to me. Guess he's given up on watching the Lions get their butts kicked again.

"Next week sometime. I want to spend some time with Zade before I go." I pull out my phone and open the app for Expedia. "Guess I should book a flight and let my mom know I'm coming home."

"I vote for surprising her," Beckett says. "Seriously, imagine how excited she'll be that you're home."

My heart kicks up. "She would be excited if I surprised her," I say, a smile pulling at my lips. I just wish I knew Gabby would be excited to see me, too.

The "Welcome to Piney Brook" sign comes into view, and I grin. It's been too long since I've been home for real. I decided to take Beckett's advice and surprise Mom, so I grabbed a rental when I landed at Northwest Arkansas National Airport.

The drive down Main Street is like going through a time machine. Not much has changed in six years. I hang a right and turn down Highway 1 toward home. I roll down the window, letting the warm spring breeze slide through the car and soothe my soul. Being stationed in Kentucky was nice, but man am I glad to be home. The thought makes me pause. Is Piney Brook still home? I don't know anymore.

I pull up to the townhouse I've shared with Mom since I was a little boy and frown. The house could use a fresh coat of paint and, from the looks of it, a few repairs. Putting the car in park, I turn off the engine and take a deep breath. This is it.

Before I have a chance to unfold myself from the little rental, Mom's at the front door. "Heath, is that you?" Her frail frame is covered in a knitted blanket, outlining just how much weight she's lost throughout the treatments.

I nod. "Hi, Ma. I'm home." I close the car door and rush up the sidewalk to catch her in my arms.

"I can't believe it," she says, tears gliding down her thin cheeks. "You're really here."

I kiss her cheek gently, and let her down. "I am. For good, or at least for a while," I say, running my hand through my hair. "How are you feeling?"

I take in the knitted cap she has on her head, the drawn-on eyebrows, and how fragile she looks. My heart breaks for her. The strongest woman I've ever known is fighting a battle we couldn't have dreamed of.

"I'm all right." She pats my hand before tucking her arm through mine and leading me into the house. "Some days are better than others."

I nod, like I have any idea how hard it's been for her. Shame eats at my gut and makes me feel like I might be physically ill. "I'm here now. I can help. You just tell me what you need."

Tears fill her eyes, and she blinks them away. "Where are Olivia and Zade?" she asks, looking in the empty car.

I grin and pull out my phone to show her the pictures I took of Zade and me at the zoo last week. "You know Zade's busy in school, and Olivia and Dominic are trying to settle into a new routine." It had taken Dominic a few years to put his head on straight and see what was right in front of him. Once he realized Olivia was pregnant, and it was his baby, he stepped up for Zade. Doing the bare minimum anyway. It wasn't until Zade had a health scare a year ago that he finally realized what he was missing out on.

"Yes, well, I'm glad that young man got it together. Even if it did take him a while." Mom gives a curt nod of her head. She was madder than a wet hen when she found out about Olivia's situation. Thankfully, she supported me helping Olivia out when she needed a friend. "They were lucky to have you to pick up the slack." She turns and walks back into the house and into the living room.

She sits down in the rocking recliner I got her the summer before I left for bootcamp, and pulls the lever, bringing the footrest up. "I was just getting ready to make some lunch, but now that you're here, I think I'd rather have something from Beats and Eats. Can you be a dear and pick us up some BLTs and fries? I've been craving that." She leans her head back and closes her eyes.

My back stiffens at the thought of going into the diner. Especially so soon after getting home. "Sure, Ma. Whatever you'd like." I just hope Gabby isn't there or this could be a disaster.

"Thanks, Heath. I'm just going to close my eyes for a few minutes while you go."

I lean in and give her a kiss on the cheek. "I'll be right back."

Fifteen minutes later, I'm circling the parking lot of Beats and Eats for the third time before I finally find a parking spot. Looks like Ms. Daisy's diner is still the place to go after church.

I slip out of the car and push the keys—and my hands—into my pockets. I spot Gabby through the window, placing food on a tray, and come to a stop.

My heart hammers in my chest. She's just as beautiful as she was the day I left. I take a deep breath and force myself to walk to the front doors.

I pull open the heavy wooden door and step inside. Beats and Eats still smells and looks exactly the same. I see some people I recognize and give a little wave, smiling when they wave back. The chatter slowly dies down as people poke each other and point to me. Great. Not quite the entrance I hoped to make, and exactly the reason I stayed out of sight during my last visit.

"Well, if it isn't little Heath Atkins," Ms. Daisy calls as she comes toward the hostess stand. A crash sounds to the left, and I see Gabby standing there, spilled food and broken plates at her feet. Her mouth hangs open like a cartoon character. Another woman steps up and whispers to her before Gabby slips into the back.

Well, that could have gone better.

CHAPTER TWO

Gabby

"Food's up," Ricky calls from behind the cook's line. I grab a tray and start gathering the plates. It's busy, even for a Sunday afternoon. Ms. Daisy opens the cafe on Sundays at eleven after morning church, and we usually draw a big crowd.

"Thanks, Ricky," I say, balancing the tray on my hand and nodding towards the front. "Looks like the wait is starting to dwindle."

He grins and flips the spatula he's holding in the air. "Don't jinx us now!"

I'm just rounding the corner when the chatter from the diners becomes quiet.

"Well, if it isn't little Heath Atkins," Ms. Daisy practically shouts.

I spin in place and come face-to-face with the only man I've ever loved. The tray slips off my hand and crashes to the floor. People start clapping, though for him or my gracefulness, I'm not sure.

"Hey, you okay?" the new girl, Patty, asks. "I've got this. Why don't you go clean up?"

I glance down at my pants. Bits of french fry and other lunch items are stuck to my clothes. Tears prick the backs of my eyes, and I nod. "Thanks," I squeak out before rushing past her and through the stainless steel swinging door that leads to the kitchen.

"Whoa," Ricky says, reaching for me. "Are you okay, Gabby? You look like you've seen a ghost." He glances through the cook's window to the front where I can still see Ms. Daisy talking with Heath.

"Yeah, I'm not feeling so well. Will you let Ms. Daisy know I had to go home early? It's slowing down, and Patty can take over for me." I untie my apron and drop it into the laundry basket Ms. Daisy keeps in the back.

"Sure," Ricky says, giving me a small smile. "Hope you feel better." He raises his eyebrows like he knows what's going on, but no one does. Not really.

I always knew he'd come back to town one day. Especially now that Mrs. A's health isn't so good. I thought I was prepared.

Guess not, Gabby. You just dropped a whole tray of food when you saw his face.

I slip out the back door and make it into my jeep without anyone stopping me. I turn the key and wait for the engine to warm up. The ole girl was my dream car, but she's finicky. Like the unbroken horse I saw down at Apple Blossom Ranch when I was a kid.

After what feels like forever, I'm finally able to ease out of the parking lot and head down the main strip towards home. I'll have to call Ms. Daisy and apologize. And I'll probably owe Patty a coffee from the Coffee Loft before our next shift together. I've never just left work like this before.

I flip on my blinker and turn into my neighborhood. Juniper Woods, where my Gram and Pop bought their house all those years ago, is a small subdivision just outside of the main part of town. It's a cute little area, with big ole oak trees, and front porches complete with swings.

I pull into the drive and groan. Something has gotten into the trash cans—again.

I jump out of the jeep and put my canvas bag on the little table by the front door before assessing the damage. Not as bad as last time. I look down at my food-splattered clothes and sigh. May as well pick it up now.

I unlock the front door of Gram's house. I'm not sure I'll ever be able to think of it as mine. I step inside and slip off my work shoes. I make my way through the living room and into the small kitchen at the back of the house. Opening the pantry door, I reach in for the garbage bags, but the box is empty.

Of course it is. I haven't been grocery shopping this week.

So, I decide to use the plastic grocery sacks from my last trip when I forgot my reusable totes. I snag a handful and walk back to the front door. I slip my feet into the rubber slides I keep there for running to the mailbox, and step back outside.

It takes me nearly half an hour and almost all the grocery sacks to pick up the mess. I glance at the garage door, stuck in its down position for the past year, and sigh. At first, it wasn't a big deal. The garbage cans were outside when it got stuck. Thank goodness, because they don't fit through the side door into the garage. I considered keeping the bags in the garage until trash day to avoid animals getting in it, but it stunk up the whole garage and created an ant problem. Clearing up the ants made dealing with the occasional yard mess seem worth it. Since Gram passed and left me the house, it seems like one thing after another keeps going wrong.

I'm not going to complain. I have a home—that's more than most people my age can say. So what if it's older and needs a little more TLC than I can provide right now?

I finish tossing the garbage into the outside can and push the lid on tight. "There, that ought to do it."

"Ought to do what?" a voice calls.

I jump and let out a little scream, slapping my hand to my heart. "Goodness gracious, Lacey, you scared me!"

Lacey looks at me and shakes her head. "What happened to you?"

I laugh. And then I keep laughing until I'm doing full-on belly laughs. The kind that when you see someone doing it, you worry about their sanity.

"Uh-huh," Lacey says. "It's worse than I thought." She takes my arm and guides me back to the house.

"Go take a shower and get out of . . ." She waves her hand up and down in front of me. "That. I'll start the tea."

I nod, still chuckling to myself. "Thanks, Lace."

She flicks her wrist and wrinkles her nose. "Don't thank me. Go change. You smell like hot garbage and yesterday's lunch."

"That bad?" I ask, turning to the hallway that leads to my bedroom and bathroom.

"Worse," she calls as I slip through the bedroom door.

The smell of baking cookies drags me from my room with my hair still wrapped in a towel. "You found stuff to make cookies?" I ask, surprised.

Lacey sputters and chuckles at me. "Uh, no, girl." She motions to the small counter hidden by the refrigerator. "I came prepared. I know you never have groceries."

She bumps the oven door closed with her hip, a tray of chocolate chip cookies in her oven mitt-covered hand. "Ms. Daisy called me after you hightailed it out of there."

I drop my head. "Oh, I suppose I should call her now."

Lacey places the tray on the stovetop and drops the shark-mouth oven mitt onto the counter. "No need. She understands."

I sigh. "No one understands. Not really."

Lacey stares at me long enough I start to squirm.

"Yeah . . ." she says. "I think people understand more than you want them to." She raises her eyebrow in challenge. "Now, go sit down in the living room. Tea and cookies coming right up."

I open my mouth to argue, but Lacey makes a shooing motion with her hand and pins me with her best "do as I say" look. She's a natural at this adulting thing, and ever since she started dating Knox, she's mastered the "mom" look.

I flop down onto the sofa, drag the throw blanket Mrs. A made for me onto my legs, and settle in. I glance at the mantle where Gram kept framed photos of all her special moments. Man, I miss her.

"All right," Lacey says, placing the tray of cookies on the ottoman and handing me a mug of steaming tea. "I'll be right back, then you're talking." She spins on her heel and heads back to the kitchen without giving me a chance to get a word in. This is going to be a long night.

Lifting the delicate cup to my mouth, I blow across the steaming hot liquid, pink and gray roses peaking at me from below the tea. I loved these cups as a young girl. Gram would set out finger sandwiches and Earl Grey Tea cookies, pour us each a cup of tea with honey, and we'd have a wonderful afternoon imagining ourselves having high tea with the Queen of England. I smile as I take a sip, letting the warmth and memories soothe me.

"There," Lacey says as she sits on the sofa next to me, her cup in her hand. "Now, spill it."

I debate how much to share. Seeing Heath today was a punch in the gut, for sure, but I'll be fine once he leaves town again. "I was surprised, that's all."

Lacey frowns. "I don't believe you," she says, taking a sip of her tea before leaning over and grabbing a cookie from the tray.

I shrug. "Rosie didn't tell me Heath was coming home to visit." I leave out the part where I didn't stick around to see his wife . . . baby's mother . . . *What is she exactly?* Rosie had never been clear about that, and I hadn't asked, choosing to keep as much conversation between the two of us away from *that* topic as possible.

"From what I understand, Heath's back home *for good.*" Lacey pops the rest of her cookie into her mouth, waiting for that news to sink in.

"Oh," I say, putting effort into seeming unaffected. "That's nice. I'm sure his mom will be thrilled to have them here."

"Them?" Lacey asks, confused.

I make a show of zipping my lip and throwing away the key like we did when we were kids. "Not my news to share," I say. Wondering for the first time why no one else in town seemed to know about Heath's child. "Can we just eat these cookies and watch a rom-com?" I ask, grabbing two cookies for myself. "I really don't want to think about Heath's surprise homecoming anymore."

Lacey pats my knee and smiles. "Sure. I don't have to open tomorrow, and Knox is home with Matti, so I don't need to rush. We can watch two rom-coms, really make an evening of it." She laughs and tucks her freshly dyed purple hair behind her ear.

"Maybe I'll dye my hair," I murmur as I grab the remote for the TV and pull up my streaming service. Fifteen dollars well spent, if you ask me.

"Oh, no you don't! Your hair is so pretty the way it is. Blondes have more fun. Isn't that what they say?"

I turn and pin her with a glare. "Does it look like I'm having fun?"

Lacey laughs. "Well, not yet, but you will be by the time we're done with these movies."

I settle on The Princess Bride, even though we've seen it a million times. The princess is stolen, and her long-lost love comes to save her. True love. If only love really withstood separation like it does in the movies.

CHAPTER THREE

Heath

One thing's for certain—Gabby is avoiding me. I've been home for three months, and every time I stop by the diner, she is too busy to take my order, or hiding in the back. Ms. Daisy shakes her head and pats my hand. "Give her time," she says.

Time? Time for what? She can't seriously be this upset still. Can she?

I've considered just driving to her house and trying to see her, but that seems like crossing a line. I'm not a stalker, just a man hoping to reconnect with an old . . . friend. So, I'll settle for eating at the diner once a week in hopes that she will stop avoiding me.

I give up on my burger and fries when I feel my phone vibrate in my pocket. Mom was resting this afternoon, so I figured I'd try—*again*—to get Gabby to talk to me.

Sliding my thumb across the screensaver of Zade smiling in front of the Wallaroo exhibit at the Louisville Zoo, I press the app notification that shows I've got a text.

Evan: Karlee's going to the Curly Pig with her friends tonight. Want to hang out?

Heath: Sure. You tell me when and where.

I close the text app and shove the phone back in my pocket. Picking up the check Patty left by my plate, I head to the hostess stand to pay for my lunch.

"Looking good, Ms. Daisy. I swear you haven't aged a bit since I left here."
I wink at her. Ms. Daisy's been in this town longer than most of us have
been alive. She's a central figure in Piney Brook. Most people consider her
family—not by blood, but love.

"I see you're just as much a charmer as ever," she says, handing me my
change, which I drop in the tip jar. "You know, some hurts never heal. Some
do. Either way, it takes time, and a bit of trust." She nods her head and smiles.

"Thanks for the advice, Ms. Daisy, but I'm not the one who has trouble
with trust," I say, tipping my head to her. "Oh, and thanks for lunch."

"Don't be a stranger, now," Patty calls out.

As I walk out, I glance to where Gabby is standing at another table, taking
their order. Her pen freezes on her pad, and she goes stiff as a board. Why's
that? I'd like to think it's because she's still as affected by me as I am by her.
Especially since Mom told me Gabby hasn't dated in over a year.

A few hours later, I'm sitting across from Evan at the Curly Pig. I shake my
head as the waitress drops off another Coke and a basket of fries. "Really?"
I ask, sitting back in my chair and looking around. "Isn't this weird?"

Evan shakes his head. "I can't help it—the Curly Pig is the only place to go
out in this town." He shrugs. "Besides, she's on the other side of the room
with her friends. I'm not bothering her."

I glance around again at Karlee chatting with the other women I met
the last time we went out. Right after I came home. That was a mistake. I
somehow thought going out and having a few beers would help it not sting
so much that Gabby wouldn't give me the time of day. Turns out, all it did
was irritate Evan, and leave me with a headache the next day. No thanks.

"All right, but I'm eating some of these fries." I put some on the little plate
the waitress left, and squeeze ketchup over the top, then I pop one into my
mouth.

"That's gross," Evan says, staring at the plate of drenched fries in disgust.
"Who eats their fries like that?"

I laugh and snag another fry. "Good thing you didn't enlist. The food they give you . . . let's just say it's not the best looking."

He shudders before dipping a fry into a puddle of ketchup. "Again, gross."

Thankfully, our table faces the wall of TVs, and the Outlaws game is on. "Think they have a shot at the series?"

Evan grins. "I think it's a real possibility. The new pitcher they have is doing great things this season."

When the game ends, I finish the rest of my Coke and throw some money on the table. "I'm going to head out. I've got a job interview tomorrow."

Evan nods his head. "That construction company in Lost Creek?"

"Yeah, I enjoyed working construction in the Army, and I can't imagine working a desk job and being stuck inside all day. I've already run out of things to do at Mom's house. I'm going stir crazy sitting still."

"I feel that," Evan says, tossing money onto the table. "I'm headed out too."

"You're not going to go over and tell Karlee bye?"

Evan grins and tucks his phone into his pocket. "No, I texted her. I don't want to interrupt her night."

I'm surprised. Since Evan and Karlee agreed to be a thing last month, they've been nearly inseparable. "Wow, that's mature," I say, as we head for the door.

"I'm learning," he says. "Thanks for hanging out tonight. It's been too long."

I nod in agreement. "Yeah, but it's life, right?"

Evan stops when we reach my truck. "It's weird. Before Karlee, I didn't mind doing my own thing at home alone. Now, though . . . it seems weird to not be having dinner with her, ya know?"

I shake my head. "Nah, can't say that I do. I'm happy for you, though. Karlee's a great girl."

"I guess you haven't had much time to date since you've been home, have you?" Evan asks. "How's your mom feeling now?"

"Better. She's slowly regaining her strength, and her hair is starting to grow back. It's crazy soft, and a bit curly." I laugh. "She said she's always wanted curly hair. Maybe now she'll have it."

Evan chuckles. "That sounds like the Rosie I know."

Opening my truck door, I slide inside and turn the key. "Thanks for the fries, and the company."

Evan steps away from the truck. "Good luck tomorrow."

"Thanks," I call before closing the door and putting the truck in reverse. With Mom doing better, it's time to settle in and decide if I'm staying in Piney Brook, or finding a new place to put down roots.

If I stay in Piney Brook, I know that would make Mom happy. She's not asked me directly what my plans are, but she's made it clear she hopes I'll stay. Piney Brook has always been where I saw myself growing old. Of course, I always imagined a certain blonde-haired beauty beside me. Now, though, I wonder if it wouldn't be better to move on. Being in the same town as Gabby and not being able to speak to her . . . that hurts.

The door creaks when I push it open. I hold my breath, hoping I didn't wake Mom up. She's taken to sleeping in the recliner lately.

"Heath, is that you?" Her tired voice almost brings me to my knees.

"Yeah, Ma. It's me," I call quietly. I slip my shoes off and put them in the cubby by the door. "How are you feeling?" I ask, turning on the low-light lamp in the corner of the living room. "Need anything?"

Mom shakes her head no, but points to the couch. "Sit with me a while?" she asks.

I sink down into the sofa cushions. "Of course," I say, resting my feet on the coffee table in front of me. I close my eyes and let the moments pass quietly.

"I haven't heard you say anything about Gabby since you've been back. Do you two talk when you're up at the diner?" Mom asks, breaking the silence.

"No, and I don't expect to. It's been five years. Why would she talk to me now?" I don't mention that every time I step foot in Beats and Eats, I hope this will be the time she acknowledges me.

"I know. Give her some time. Maybe now that you're home for good," Mom says, giving me a pointed look, "she'll come around."

"It's been five years, Mom. Things change. People change."

I sigh. It's been a long time since Mom brought up Gabby. After she blocked me everywhere, I sent her a letter explaining the mess with Olivia. I may have decided we should break up, but I didn't want her to think I'd cheated on her.

When I didn't hear back from her, I asked Mom to make sure she knew the whole story. After that, the ball was in her court. I had to leave her be. I'd been the one to break things off, so I didn't feel like I had the right to push her. I still don't. But I miss having her in my life. If we could just talk again, be friends—even sort of friends—I'd be happy. Well, happier anyway.

CHAPTER FOUR

Gabby

It's Sunday afternoon, and the rush has slowed down. I watch as Heath leaves the diner, finally. He's been coming in nearly every Sunday and—bless Patty's heart—she's been taking care of him every time. "I'm sorry," I say, rolling my shoulders to let go of some of the tension I've been holding. "What was that?"

I finish writing down the order for the table I'm serving, and head behind the counter to the computer to punch it in. While other restaurants in town have fancy handheld systems now, Ms. Daisy is attached to the older way of doing things. Suits me fine. I've just finished ringing in the order when she comes to stand by my side.

"Gabby, when are you going to give that boy a break?" She pats my back. "I don't know what happened exactly, but I have eyes, dear."

I shake my head. "I don't know what you're talking about," I lie. "Heath and I were friends, he left, and we drifted apart. What more is there to say?"

Ms. Daisy opens her mouth, her perfectly shaped eyebrow raised almost to her hairline. "Gabby, Gabby, Gabby . . ." She looks to the ceiling as if asking for strength. "You're more stubborn than your grandmother was, and that's saying something."

"Orders up," Ricky calls, putting four dishes into the warming window.

"I've got to run this food," I say, grateful for the interruption. I stack the plates onto a tray, double checking the order's correct.

"When have I ever messed up your order?" Ricky asks, amusement dancing in his eyes.

I shrug. "There's a first time for everything."

He laughs as I lift the tray in the air and head toward the table.

"Here we are," I say, setting the tray down on a stand and passing out the warm plates. "Is there anything else I can get you?"

"I think we're good, thank you," the woman says, leaning over to cut her child's burger in half.

"Enjoy." I take the stand and the empty tray, and put them away. Wiping my hands on my apron, I steal a glance at the clock. Almost time for my shift to be over. "I'm going to run to the back and take a minute. Is that okay?"

Patty glances at my section. "They just get their food?"

"Yep, and they should be all set. My other table has cashed out, and they are about to leave."

She nods. "Go on, then."

"Thanks," I say, taking a glass and adding ice and sweet tea to it before popping through the swinging door to the staff area in the back. I pull out a chair at the rectangular table shoved against a wall in the break room and plop down into it. My phone buzzes in my apron pocket, and I take it out.

Momma A: Are you free tonight? I'd love some company since Heath will be out with Evan.

I roll my eyes. I'm glad Heath reconnected with Evan. It seems the whole town is thrilled to have him back, and I'd be lying if I said I'm not a little relieved he's home in one piece. I just can't figure out where Zade and Olivia are, and I don't have it in me to ask. Seems the only one who knows about them is Momma A. Why would he keep his child a secret from the whole town? Maybe she's still in the Army and couldn't relocate yet. That would make sense, except I'd have expected Heath to stay with them.

Gabby: I'd love that too. I'll bring dinner—anything you want.

I stare at the phone and contemplate asking Rosie about Olivia and Zade. She was so excited to be a grandma that she gave me updates and showed me pictures all the time. At least she did until her diagnosis. I shake myself out of the funk I'm falling into when my phone buzzes in my hand.

Momma A: How about today's special from the diner?

Gabby: You've got it. Be there around 5:30.

When Heath was getting ready to leave for basic training, I could tell he was worried about his mom. "*It's been the two of us against the world for so long,*" he said. I loved spending time with his mom, working in her garden, cooking, just being. So, naturally, I said I'd be there for her. Keep her company and make sure she was okay while he was gone.

And I did.

Even when he broke my heart into a million pieces.

A while after that awful night, I went over to see Rosie, and she told me that Heath asked her to "explain" things to me. Then she told me that Olivia's baby "isn't really his;" that he was just pretending because the real daddy was her sergeant and they'd get in trouble. *Uh-huh.* I guess lying to your mom is par for the course when you're already sleeping around. Every time she'd show me little Zade's picture, I'd fight back tears. Heath and I were supposed to have a family one day.

After the facetime call that revealed the truth, I couldn't take it. I blocked his number and his email and refused to talk about him with anyone. He sent me a letter, but I chucked it. I didn't want letters from someone else's man. Thinking about it makes my jaw tense still. If he wanted to be with someone else, why wait till she was pregnant before breaking up with me?

When Momma A got her cancer diagnosis eighteen months ago, I was the one to take her to the hospital. I couldn't abandon her, not like everyone abandoned me. I was there for every appointment and treatment until Heath came home a few months ago.

"Your table is ready to check out," Patty says, poking her head through the opening of the swinging door.

Startled, I drop my phone to the floor. "I'm sorry," I say, picking it up and stuffing it back into my apron. "I didn't realize I'd been back here so long."

Patty smiles. "It's no problem. Ms. Daisy said to let you know you're cut for the day."

"Thanks." I smooth my apron down and take a deep breath before pushing through the door to the dining room. After giving my table their bill, and making sure they had to-go boxes, I did my side work, and clocked out.

"Ms. Daisy, can I get two specials to go, please?"

She smiles. "Are you visiting Rosanna tonight?"

I nod. "She messaged and asked if I'd like to come over." Ms. Daisy is the town mom, grandma, advice giver, aunt . . . whatever you need her to be. She is something special, and I know it. I love working for her.

"On the house," she says, handing me a bag with the hot, wholesome smell of fried chicken wafting from it. "I threw in some dessert, too." I open my mouth to argue, but she continues talking over my protest. "You just tell Rosie that I'm thinking of her, ya hear?"

I nod and lean in to give her a quick hug. "I hear."

I pull into the drive, noticing again how sad the front garden is looking. I make a mental note to come by and refresh the flower beds. She loves a colorful front walkway.

I make my way up the steps to the front door and ring the bell. The front door swings open, and Heath is standing there in sweatpants and a t-shirt. His eyes widen as he takes me in. "Gabby." He whispers my name like a prayer. As though I might disappear.

"There you are," calls Rosie from behind him. "Come in, dear. Come in. Don't block the doorway, Heath. Where are your manners?"

Heath steps back and motions for me to come inside, a grin tugging at the corner of his lips. My mouth goes dry, remembering for a moment how soft his lips had been on mine that summer.

"I hope you don't mind," Rosie's saying. "Seems I got my days mixed up, and Heath was staying home tonight." She looks at me with a sparkle in her eye, and it dawns on me that I've been set up.

Heath glances from me to his mom, before tipping his head to the side and pointing a finger in her direction. "Mom, did you invite Gabby here under false pretenses?"

Momma A gasps and draws back, her hand fluttering to her chest. "Why, I never! Heath Josiah Atkins, what a thing to suggest."

I'd almost buy it if she wasn't fighting a smile.

"Honestly, you've gotten my blood pressure up. I need to lie down. You don't mind, do you, dear?" she asks, pinning me with a look that leaves no room for argument. "I'd hate for that food to go to waste, but I just don't think I'll be able to eat a bite tonight. You two go ahead without me."

Before I can respond, she hugs me, kisses Heath's cheek, then turns and trudges down the hall.

"I'm sorry," Heath says, watching as his mom closes her bedroom door. "I didn't know she'd invited you over."

I stare at him for a moment. It's clear he's just as surprised by this turn of events as I am. "It's okay. I'll leave the food and go. I'm sure Ms. Daisy's fried chicken will reheat well." I put the bag down on the coffee table and make my way back toward the front door. Heath follows and speaks to my back.

"Gabby, wait. I've never gotten to thank you for all you've done for my mom. It's meant so much to me to know that you were here caring for her while she's been sick. I'm so grateful to you for all of the hours you've spent with her. Thank you."

I soften a little, letting my shoulders relax a fraction. I talk to the door as I answer.

"You're welcome. It was my pleasure to repay some of the kindness she's shown me for years. I love your mom. Tell her goodbye for me." I turn the knob, but the door doesn't open. Heath's hand is holding it closed.

"Please, stay." His voice is soft, pleading.

I close my eyes, tears welling up behind my lids. "I don't think that's a good idea."

"Please. One hour. Eat the meal you brought." He takes his hand from the door.

I shake my head and open the door. "I can't." Tears are falling down my face before I even step off the front landing.

"Why?" Heath asks. "I know we broke up, but we were best friends, and I never intended for that to end. I've missed you so much. You stopped taking my calls. You never wrote me back. Don't I deserve to know why?" His voice is soft, sad even. "Please?"

I gasp and spin on my heel. "You *deserve? You* deserve?" I hiss, barely holding my temper in check. "You dumped me and *then* I find out you already fathered a child with some other woman and didn't have the nerve to tell me yourself. You broke my heart," I say, poking him in the chest. "Did I deserve *that*, Heath?"

He shakes his head and lifts his hands to my shoulders. "Gabby, my mom told you the truth about the baby, didn't she?"

I shake my head. "She told me the story you told her. You expect me to believe that? Listen, I got over you a long time ago, so just let me be, and I'll do the same for you."

He pulls me into him and wraps his arms around me. I sink into his warmth for a moment before realizing my mistake. "Gabby, he's not mine." I pull out of his arms and rush to the car.

I freeze as I open the car door. "What good is it to lie to me still? You broke up with me to be with her, so go be with her. You don't need me."

"Please, can we talk?" Heath asks from behind me.

I let out a breath. "Why? What difference does it make now, Heath?"

"Because I still love you," he says, just loud enough for me to hear him.

A sob breaks from my chest and I open the car door and slide in. "You can't," I say, shaking my head no. "Don't say that. Don't treat Olivia the way you treated me. You'll break your mom's heart. Zade and Olivia are all she can talk about. She is so proud to be a grandmother."

He nods his head. "*Honorary* grandmother, Gabby. Zade was never mine. It was never a question. I let people believe he was to help a friend, that's all."

"Yeah. I heard that. And, what, now you and your *friend* Olivia are breaking up, so you'll settle for me? Good job sticking to your story, but I don't want to be the *other woman* in your life. I want you to leave me alone." I give him one last lingering glance, close the car door, and drive away.

Back at home, I sit on the couch, clutching a throw pillow to my chest. I've replayed his words a thousand times, and they're still swimming around in my head. The whole time I knew Heath, he'd never lied. Not even to get out of trouble. Why would he make up that story?

And Rosanna believes him. Wouldn't she have found out the truth by now? Maybe I've been holding onto this anger for all the wrong reasons.

But whether or not the story's true, why did he break up with me? Was he just not in love with me? Maybe he got that distance between us and decided his life was better without me.

The worst part is I still miss him. I miss talking to him . . . He was my best friend, even before we acknowledged we had deeper feelings.

A knock at the door saves me from that train of thought. I use my shirt to wipe the trail of tears off of my face. "Coming," I call out.

CHAPTER FIVE

Heath

I stand in the front yard watching Gabby pull away. All this time she thought I was lying? I shake my head. I'd let myself be dragged into an impossible situation, and was naive enough at the time to think it wouldn't backfire.

If I'd known then . . . I think of Olivia and Zade. If I'd known then, I would have made sure that Gabby knew the truth before she found out from some idiot jokester like she had. Hands down, I would have still tried to help Olivia. I couldn't just leave a single mom to handle everything on her own. That's just not who I am.

I turn and make my way back inside. I close the door softly behind me and lean back against it, banging my head in frustration a couple of times.

"So," Mom's voice calls from the kitchen. "I take it you two didn't work it out?" She sounds disappointed, but there's no one more disappointed than me. Somehow I'd thought we would eventually talk and I could convince her to let me back into her life.

"No, I guess not," I say, walking into the kitchen and taking a seat at the table. "She thinks I lied about Zade and Olivia," I say, still a bit shocked by that revelation. "All this time, she thought . . ." I lean forward, resting my arms on the table in front of me. "I messed up."

Mom takes a bite of fried chicken and hums. "Everyone messes up. It's how you make it right that matters."

I drop my head onto my arms. "What if she doesn't want to make it right?" I close my eyes and will my heart to stop breaking again.

"Then you start over. You earn her trust." Mom drops this bit of advice like it's just that easy.

"Start over?" I ask, raising my head to look at her. "How?"

"Show her you want to be her friend." She shrugs. "You two were friends before you were anything more. That's where you need to start again. Time has passed, you've both grown and changed. The wishes of two kids barely old enough to vote may not measure up to the dreams you have as adults."

"I'll think about it. I'm going to bed," I say, pushing the chair back. "I love you, Ma. But no more meddling." I hold her gaze and can't help but soften. "Night."

She nods her head. "I know. You two just needed a push. I'll stay out of it. Goodnight, son. I love you."

Monday morning, I'm in a small office sitting across from Allen Davis, owner of Lost Creek Construction. Now that I know Mom's treatments are over and she's getting stronger, it's time for me to get a job. My old buddy Tim works for them; he saw me out at the Curly Pig, and let me know they were always looking for good workers. I finally took the initiative and sent in an application. I was called in for an interview a few days later, but he had a family emergency and had to reschedule to today.

I rub my hands on my jeans. I'm nervous, and I don't know why. After the things I've done, places I've been—this is cake.

"You were in the Army," Allen says. "You didn't want to re-enlist?"

I shake my head. "No, my mom got sick while I was deployed. Cancer. She's all right now, but it made me realize I wanted to be back home. When my term was up, I decided to get out."

"Sorry to hear about your mom, son," he says, sympathy pouring off of him in waves. It almost suffocates me. "Cancer's tough."

I nod, unsure of what else to say.

"Do you have any construction experience?"

"I do. I was a Carpentry and Masonry Specialist. I learned a lot, but I'm sure there's more I can pick up along the way. I'm a fast learner, and determined. I like working with my hands. I didn't want to come home and work a desk job."

"Sounds like you'd be a great addition to the company." Allen grins. "I think we can get you started soon. I have two crews. One works over here in Lost Creek mainly. That team is headed up by Tim Miller. The other team's lead is Bradley Turner, and they're over towards the Piney Brook area."

"I can work wherever I'm needed, sir." I hold my breath. While I *can* work wherever I'm needed, I'd love to be on the crew closer to home.

Allen eyes me for a minute, then picks up his phone and makes a call. "Hey, Bradley, it's Allen." He pauses a beat. "Good, good. Listen, I have a new guy. Army. I'm sending him your way." He chuckles and winks at me. "Nah, tomorrow. He'll be filling out the paperwork today. Thanks, Bradley."

He hangs up the phone and grabs a clipboard that's resting on the side of his desk. Passing it over to me, he smiles. "Welcome to the team."

"Thank you, sir. I appreciate it."

I spend the rest of the afternoon filling out new hire paperwork and watching job safety videos. At five o'clock, Tim steps in. "I see you got yourself a job." He shakes my hand. "Too bad you're not on my crew."

"Not going to lie, I'm happy to be closer to home. With Mom . . . well, I'll feel better knowing I'm not so far out."

Tim nods. "I understand. Forty-five minutes can seem like forever sometimes." He steps up to the wall and hangs his clipboard up on a hook. "It's quitting time. Feel like heading out for a burger with the guys?"

I pull out my phone. No missed calls or messages. "Sure, that sounds great."

I check in with Allen before hopping into my truck and following Tim to a rustic-looking building with a gravel lot. The white-and-green sign at the entrance says "McFaddens." We step inside, and I see the rustic theme is carried throughout. Wooden tables and chairs take up most of the center. A mechanical bull is off to the right in the back, near the restrooms. There's country music playing over the speakers, and peanut shells on the floor.

"Best burgers in town," Tim says, looking around. He seems to spot who he's looking for in the corner booth opposite the bull. "Come on, they're here."

I follow him to the large table in the back of the room. I slide into an open seat, and look around.

"This is Heath. He's joining Brad's team over in Piney Brook," Tim says by way of introduction.

I give a little wave. "Hey."

"I'm Reid," the only man dressed in slacks and a button-up says. "This knucklehead doesn't know how to give proper introductions." He tosses a wadded up napkin at Tim, who's already lost in the menu. "This is Dustin, Levi, and Jack."

"Nice to meet you," I say, a little unsure of myself. "So, what's good?" I ask, trying to break the tension.

Dustin laughs. "Everything. Seriously, you can't go wrong here."

I open the menu and scan the options. Burgers, steaks, wings . . . Everything looks good.

"Hey there," a waitress says, setting cocktail napkins on the table in front of me and Tim. "What can I get you to drink?"

"I'll have a water, please," I say when it's my turn.

"Y'all ready to order your food?" she asks the table. Everyone takes turns giving their order, and the waitress collects the menus and walks away.

"I hope I don't regret ordering the double bacon burger," I say, patting my stomach.

"No way," Levi says from the other end of the table. "That's my favorite."

The guys get lost in conversation about the job site they are working on, and I listen, taking it all in. They barely pause when the food is delivered, jumping right back into their banter. It reminds me of the mess hall during basic. Everyone is eager to offload their frustrations of the day. I didn't realize it until this moment, but I've been missing the camaraderie. I just hope the crew I'm assigned to is this friendly.

—*ell*—

"Well, how was it?" Mom asks the minute I step through the door.

I slide off my shoes and head toward the kitchen for some water. "It was good. I got the job. I'll be on the crew that mainly works in Piney Brook."

Mom claps her hands together. "That's wonderful news!"

I grab a glass from the cabinet and fill it at the sink. "It is. I'm ready to get settled. Figure out if I'm staying in Piney Brook long term, you know?"

Her face falls. "I'd always dreamed of you living close by, but I understand. You're grown now. You'll make the best decision for yourself."

I push off the counter I'd been leaning on, put the glass down on the counter, and pull her in for a hug. "I didn't say I was leaving, Ma."

She sniffles. "I know. I'm sorry. I just missed you so much while you were gone. I never did get used to it."

I smile and hold her a little tighter, careful not to squeeze too hard. "Me either," I say.

"When do you start?" she asks, stepping out of my arms and changing the subject.

"Tomorrow. I'll meet up with Bradley Turner's crew downtown. They're starting some renovations for a local business down there."

"Oh," Mom says. "I bet they're the ones doing the renovations for the Coffee Loft."

I shrug. "I don't know, I didn't ask. Did you eat?"

Mom smiles. "I did. I went to the diner and ate with Ms. Daisy. That woman knows just about everything there is to know in the town." She shakes her head. "You'd think she was the town hair stylist, for all the stuff people share with her."

I run my hands through my shaggy hair. "Speaking of," I say. "Who is the town stylist these days? I should get this trimmed at least."

Mom laughs. "I was wondering if you were boycotting hair cuts now that you're out of the Army."

"Not really," I say. "Just wanted to grow it out a bit."

"Well, Anne is running Master Cuts now that her aunt has retired. She does a great job."

"Anne Masters? From school?" I ask. I remember Anne. She was in the same grade as me. Tiny thing with big ole braces. "I haven't seen her in years. I thought she'd leave town and head to New York or California. Someplace fancy."

Mom shakes her head. "She left for school, but then decided she wanted to come back. I guess big city life isn't what it's cracked up to be."

I nod. "I know that's the truth. Piney Brook is special. You can leave, but a part of you will always stay." I may have traveled the world, but my heart was always here. In Gabrielle Fineman's hands.

CHAPTER SIX

Gabby

I lie in bed and pull the sheets over my head. The late summer means the house has a bit of a chill in the mornings. Of course, sleeping with the windows open might have something to do with it. The soft sound of mockingbirds calling for the sun to rise brings a small smile to my face. There's a nest in the tree outside my window and waking up to their serenade makes me smile every day.

I cuddle into the sheets and close my eyes. It's my day off. I've got an appointment with Anne this afternoon, but I'm gloriously free until then. My phone chimes with an incoming message, and I groan. I'm not answering it.

It dings again, and I give up. Rolling over, I reach a hand from beneath the covers and feel around until I grab it. Pulling the phone into my cocoon, I swipe it open and see three missed texts.

Two from Lacey, and one from Momma A. I'll open that one last. Lacey seriously texted me twice reminding me to come in for the Apple Crisp Frappuccino the Coffee Loft just added to the menu. I shake my head. It will be here all fall. I have several months to try the newest creation.

Taking a breath, I open the message from Momma A.

Momma A: I'm throwing a birthday party for Heath. I'd love it if you would come.

I drop my phone beside me and close my eyes.

I keep thinking about our conversation the other night, and I've started to wonder if I'm being too judgmental. Yeah, so he broke my heart—that was a long time ago. How he chooses to live his life doesn't have anything to do with me anymore. We were friends once.

Besides Lacey, Heath was the only other person I felt truly myself with. I didn't have to pretend that my family life was something it wasn't. That my mom didn't abandon me for her latest fling. He listened. He saw me.

We could be friends again, right? Maybe he'll eventually open up to me and I'll finally know the truth. So much time has passed, it would be like starting over in a way. Can I handle that? Especially when for so long it's felt like he abandoned me, threw me over for someone new. Just like my mom did.

Unless . . .

What if it is the truth? What if he really isn't the father and he's not with Olivia? That would mean that he broke up with me because he just wasn't in love with me anymore. I need to know more before I can figure this out. But knowing more would require talking to him, and trusting him again.

I miss talking to him, being understood and seen by him, but I'm not sure I can let him in again, even as friends.

I push back the covers and swing my legs over the side of the bed. I can't make decisions like this without some coffee first.

Thirty minutes later, I'm standing in line at the Coffee Loft when someone taps my shoulder. Turning around, I see Momma A, a wide grin on her face.

"I was hoping to bump into you today, but when I went to the diner, Ms. Daisy told me it's your day off."

I lean in and give her a hug. "It's great to see you out and about. How are you feeling?" I take in her short hair, and perfectly done makeup. For a moment I feel bad that I've not been spending as much time with her as I used to. *She doesn't need me anymore*, I remind myself. *Heath's home.*

"I'm feeling good," she says, patting her do. "The hair's coming back in nicely, and the doctors say my scans are promising."

"That's wonderful!" It truly is. Thankfully, when she noticed the small lump, her doctors took her seriously and had it checked out.

"Care to join me for a cup?" she asks, pointing to the menu. "My treat."

I smile. "I'll join you on one condition," I say. "*My* treat."

We step up to the counter, and Lacey greets us both. "What can I get you two beautiful women today?"

Momma A blushes. "You sure know how to make an old lady feel good."

I scoff. "You're hardly an old lady, Rosie. You're not a day over twenty-nine I'm told."

She laughs. "You know, Heath didn't know how old I was until his senior year in highschool when he finally did the math. He just happily went along celebrating my twenty-ninth birthday each year."

I chuckle. "I remember. You might need to switch decades here in the next while. It'll get confusing for people when your son passes you up." Rosie and I laugh. I'm still smiling when I turn and give Lacey my order. "I'll take a Lofty Apple Crisp Frappuccino. What about you?"

Rosie gives hers, and I pay the tab. "Let's find a seat."

"How about that one by the window?" Momma A asks, making her way over there. "I just love being near the sunshine."

I follow her to the table and pull out the seat across from her. "Me too."

"So," we say at the same time, then giggle. I motion for her to talk first.

"So," she starts again. "Did you get my text?"

"I did," I say as Lacey places the coffee on the table in front of us. "Thanks, Lacey."

"You got it," she says cheerfully before heading back behind the counter.

"Well?" Rosie asks as she takes a sip of her coffee. "Do you think you can make it?"

I quickly take a sip of my drink. Sweet, but not too sweet. Just the way I like it. I make a mental note to tell Lacey it's been moved up on my fall favorites list, just behind the tried-and-true Pumpkin Spice Latte. "I'm not sure," I finally say. "I'll have to check my schedule."

Rosie grins. "I cleared the day with Daisy already. I wanted to make sure I picked a day you could make it."

My smile falters. Darn that Ms. Daisy. There goes my out. If I say no now, it would hurt Momma A's feelings. "Oh, that's good."

"So, you'll come?" Rosie hasn't taken her eyes off of me, and it makes it impossible to let her down.

"I'll be there. Do you need help with anything?" I find myself asking. Mentally, I kick myself. I don't need to be offering help. This isn't my responsibility.

"Nope, I've got it covered. Thanks, though."

We spend the next few minutes talking about the weather, and her doctor's appointments before she stands and tells me goodbye. The moment the door swings shut behind her, Lacey is at the table.

"So, what did you think?" she asks, pointing to my nearly empty cup.

"It was good," I say. "It's definitely in my top five fall flavors."

Lacey does a happy dance. "Aurora and I picked them out together. Every Coffee Loft has their own spin on flavors. Aurora didn't choose a signature flavor last year because we were all trying to learn the basics, but this year she decided it was time. I'm excited to try out some new things this season."

"Well, you chose a good one," I say, smiling at her enthusiasm. "Any word on when you'll be able to open the center?" Lacey had come back to Piney Brook with dreams of opening an early childhood enrichment center.

"Should be soon," she says. "The construction crew has started on the renovations already. Though there was a small hiccup when Aurora saw who the foreman was." She laughs. "Apparently, there's some history there. I reminded her that my wish was coming true, and she could just ignore Bradley until it's over. She finally relented."

I cringe. *Not all wishes come true.*

"How's that working out?" I know from experience it's hard to ignore someone you have a history with.

Lacey grins. "I think he still has a thing for her, but for now, it seems they've called a truce of sorts."

"That's good at least," I say, realizing I should do the same. Ignoring Heath isn't helping me get over him, and I'd prefer things not be so weird all the time.

"It's so nice to see Mrs. A out and about again." Lacey picks up her empty mug. "She seemed excited to see you."

"It is good that she's out. I haven't been spending as much time over there since Heath's been home. It was nice to see her and catch up for a few minutes."

Lacey looks at me curiously. "Did you ask her about his kid?"

I look around the nearly empty dining area. "Have a minute?" I ask.

"Ash, I'm taking a break," she calls out.

"You got it," Ashlan says.

"I have all the time in the world," Lacey says, pulling out the chair Momma A was just sitting in.

"Remember when Heath and I stopped talking?" I ask. Lacey nods her head and leans into the table. "Well, he had his mom talk to me. She said that Heath was helping out a friend, and the baby wasn't his. At the time, I was convinced he'd lied to his mom. You know how she would feel about having a baby out of wedlock. She's always said marriage first, then babies."

"Okay, and now?" Lacey asks.

"Now I'm not so sure. Why would he be back here without his child? Why would he keep that lie up for so long?" I shake my head. "I don't know what to think anymore."

"Oh my goodness," Lacey says, shaking her head. "That's a lot to process."

I nod. "You're not wrong."

"Heath never struck me as the type to lie about things," Lacey says.

"That's just it. He didn't seem like the type to break my heart either, but he did." I blush—saying it out loud for the first time, even to my best friend, is a lot.

"You two were so young," Lacey says, reaching out and patting my hand. "Do you still have feelings for him?"

Do I? I thought I'd moved on, but having him here in Piney Brook again . . . "I think I might," I answer honestly.

"So, you two talked. Are you friends again?"

"I don't know," I say, truthfully. "A lot of time has passed. We haven't been friends in years."

"But that was your choice, right?" she asks.

"It was. I thought he needed to be focused on starting that next part of his life, not tied to Piney Brook. Well, besides his mom, I suppose." I pick at the peeling polish on my thumb nail. Mentally adding a manicure to my to-do list today.

Lacey nods. "Okay, but you two were so close after graduation. People sort of assumed you two would end up together."

I shrug. "People always make assumptions, doesn't always make them right." I hear those words play again in my head and my throat goes dry. I've been assuming a lot about Heath for a long time. I may have been wrong all this time. If so, he must think I'm an idiot.

She looks at me, and I squirm in my seat. "Sometimes things aren't meant to be."

"And sometimes, when things *are* meant to be, you get a second chance. Have you considered that?"

I laugh. "Not everything is a Hallmark movie or a romance novel, Lace."

"I still think you should at least try to be friends again." Her eyes go wide as the door opens behind me. "Speaking of Heath . . ."

I turn in time to see the moment he spots me. His eyes flicker with recognition and something that looks like sadness. He's dressed in jeans and a pair of work boots, and a blue t-shirt with "Lost Creek Construction" across the chest in white lettering. Makes sense he'd get a job working with his hands. Heath hated school, couldn't wait to get out of a desk and make something of himself.

I smile a little and raise my hand to wave. A peace offering of sorts. Lacey's right. We were friends once. What could it hurt to be friends again?

CHAPTER SEVEN

Heath

Seeing Gabby sitting in the Coffee Loft takes my breath away. She lifts her hand and gives me a little wave. My heart stutters to a stop in my chest. I raise my hand in a lame attempt to wave back. Why did things between us have to get so awkward? Oh, that's right . . . I decided to break up with the girl I loved and she thought I'd dumped her for someone else.

Turning away from her is difficult, but I promised the crew I'd pick up some muffins and coffee. "Can I get a large to-go box of regular coffee, and six of your muffins please?" I ask the pretty girl behind the counter.

"Sure thing," she says, entering the order and stepping away. "You're with Bradley's crew, right?"

I nod. Realizing she can't see me, I clear my throat and answer. "Yeah, just started on with them."

She finishes boxing the muffins and moves to the coffee station where she makes quick work of filling a massive to-go container with heavenly caffeine. "Making the new guy run the errands, I see."

I smile. "I offered. I was getting hungry, and honestly, I could use the pick me up."

She wipes her hands on a towel she has hanging from her apron. "That will be $47.50."

I slip my wallet from my back pocket and take out three twenty-dollar bills. "Keep the change."

"Thanks!" She grins and tucks the money into the register before putting the change in a jar labeled tips. "We appreciate it."

I nod. "See ya," I say, grabbing the coffee and muffins. I resist walking to where Gabby and Lacey are talking at a table in front of the window, deciding instead to play it cool. "See ya later, Gabby. Lacey."

I push through the doors and onto the sidewalk before they can reply. *There, that wasn't so hard. It's not like I told her I'd never gotten over her.*

I walk the three feet to the job site next door. Turns out we are working on a play center or something of the like. Since starting on with Bradley a few weeks ago, I'd like to think I've found my footing. The crew is nice. Most of the guys are married. Only Bradley, myself, and Hudson are still single, at least on the Piney Brook team. Though I get the feeling both of them have their hearts, or at least their sights, set on someone already.

Setting the coffee and muffins down on the makeshift lunch table, I call out, "Coffee's here." I don't wait to see if anyone heard me. Filling up my cup, I grab a muffin and move to a cleanish spot in what will be the lobby and check-in area, and slide down the wall to sit on the floor.

The space is big, with lots of windows already in place. The architect, Reid, who drew up the designs, left the exterior pretty much alone. Choosing instead to focus the budget on the interior of the building. It's going to be nice. Once we've finished with the inside, we'll be connecting this side with the Coffee Loft next door. Pretty smart if you ask me. Giving parents a way to grab coffee and a snack while their kids take in a class or play.

"You going to get any work done today, Heath?" Bradley asks, lifting his muffin in the air and grinning. "Or are you planning to sit around all day?"

The guys all laugh, and it makes me grin. Teasing is part of the job, part of being in the crew. I've missed that since coming home from the Army.

"I was just waiting for my nails to dry," I say, laughing at my own bad pun. Bradley shakes his head and nudges Hudson. "This guy thinks he's funny."

Hudson stuffs the rest of the muffin he's been eating into his mouth and swallows. "If he keeps bringing muffins, he can make all the jokes he wants." He points his hard hat at me and grins. "Next time, see if they have any blueberry. Those are my favorite." He puts his hat back on his head and goes back to work.

The rest of the day passes in a blur of power tools and sweat. Wiping my arm across my forehead, I sigh. We stand outside the building while Bradley locks up. "You want to go to Daisy's with us?" he asks.

I shake my head. "Not tonight, I'm beat." I don't want to go into the diner looking like I rolled around the floor of the jobsite all day, and smelling even worse. I subtly try to sniff my armpits and flinch. The weather is starting to cool off slightly, but it doesn't erase the smell of a hard day's work. "I'm going to head home, shower, and hit the sack. Y'all have fun, though."

Bradley nods. "Your loss. It's fried chicken night."

Ms. Daisy's has some of the best fried chicken in all of Northwest Arkansas, and for a second, I debate going. "Have a piece for me," I say, choosing to stick to my original plan.

I climb in my truck and roll down the window to wave as I pull out of the parking lot and head home.

The minute I walk through the front door, Mom motions for me to have a seat in the dining room. She sets a plate of meatloaf, mashed potatoes and broccoli in front of me. "Heath, you'll be home this Saturday, right?" Mom asks, putting on her most innocent face.

I groan, putting down my fork. "What are you up to? Do I even want to know?"

She smiles, and bats her eyelashes like a southern belle debutante at her coming-out ball. "Heath, why on earth do you think I'm up to something? Can't I just want to spend time with my son?"

I raise an eyebrow and pin her with the same stare she used to give me when I was a kid causing trouble. "Mm-hmm."

"So, you'll be home, then?"

I nod. "I don't have plans, if that's what you're asking."

She claps her hands together and grins. "I can't wait to spend the day with you."

"Me too," I say, picking up my fork to finish my dinner. Once I've cleaned the plate, I take it to the sink and rinse it before putting my dirty dishes into the dishwasher. "It's been a long day, Ma. I'm going to head to bed."

She nods and heads back to the living room. I watch as she slides back into the recliner and picks up her knitting needles. She's taken to knitting hats for other people at the cancer center. Stylish little head covers for others who are dealing with hair loss and cancer treatments. It hits me how strong she's been. Not just now, but my whole life. "I love you," I call before heading down the hall and into my room. I could use a good night's sleep. Running into Gabby today had me working hard to keep my mind off of her. I'm beat.

The next morning, I'm awake bright and early. I make Mom some breakfast and brew a pot of coffee before grabbing my keys and heading into work. I'm clocked in and hanging drywall in one of the rooms that will become a classroom when I hear a ruckus in the main part of the building. I finish screwing in the piece I'm working on and head out front to see what the commotion is about.

I step through the doorway separating the lobby from the back classroom area and lose my breath. Gabby is standing in the doorway with a huge to-go tote of coffee and an assortment of muffins.

"Gabby?" Surprise roots my feet to the floor.

She waves. "Hey, I thought y'all could use some coffee today." She looks so cute bundled up in her long coat and knee-high boots, a burnt orange scarf wrapped around her neck. Her hair is shorter than it was yesterday. It looks good on her. "It's a cold one," she says, reminding me that I can't just stand here staring at her.

"Thanks." I really want to ask why she's here, but I don't dare. I don't want to spook her.

"Well, don't leave her standing there with her hands full," Hudson says, stepping over to take the muffin box. Lifting it open, he grins. "Blueberry!"

She grins and tucks a strand of hair behind her ear. "They're my favorite."

I make a mental note of that information. Stepping forward, I take the coffee box from her hand and place it on the table. "Thanks again," I say, slipping my hands into my pockets so I don't reach for her.

"Do you have a minute?" she asks, rocking back on her heels.

My heart tugs with hope. "Yeah, I can probably take a break." I turn to find Bradley. He's already filling a cup of coffee.

"Go," he says, snagging a muffin. "You started before everyone else today, anyway."

I nod and motion for Gabby to lead the way. She steps out the front door and moves down the sidewalk to a bench that overlooks the grassy area in the middle of downtown. She sits and waits for me to take my place next to her.

"I'm sorry I've been avoiding you. I've been going over our conversation and I realize I was thinking wrong this whole time. If I'd known the truth from the beginning, I still don't know if I would have stayed in contact with you—you did break up with me. We had a plan back then, and I was all in," she says. "When you broke it off, I was hurt. I didn't just lose a boyfriend back then, I lost one of my best friends."

I nod. "Me too. Well, not the boyfriend part, but I lost my best friend, too."

She gives me a half smile for my joke, and looks up from under her lashes. "I was hoping . . ." She pauses, and my breath catches in my throat.

Please be hoping we can start again. Please! "Yes?" I ask, as calmly as I can manage. I want to lean in and press my lips to hers. See if she still tastes as sweet as I remember in my dreams. When I catch my gaze dropping to her mouth, I force it back to her eyes.

"I was hoping we could be friends. Talking to your mom the other day made me realize this town's not big enough to keep avoiding each other forever."

I swallow hard. Friends. That's *something*. When I was away, I didn't just miss having her for a girlfriend. I missed *her*. Talking and laughing about dumb things, and sharing deep secrets and hard memories. Having her in my life again in any form would be a blessing. "Friends, like we were before?"

She shakes her head. "More like acquaintances. I don't want to feel like I can't visit your mom or see you around town without freezing up. So, friendly acquaintances?"

I rub my hands on my jeans to keep from taking her hands in mine. "If that's what you want," I say, trying to hide my hurt. I know I hurt her, but I was hurt, too. If I could turn back time . . .

"Good," she says, standing. She sticks out her hand for me to shake. "To being friends."

I shake her hand, hoping my face doesn't give me away. "Friends."

CHAPTER EIGHT

Gabby

Heath shakes my hand, and it feels . . . wrong. I woke up this morning determined to make things, not *right*, but better. I didn't want to go to his birthday party this weekend with things still so awkward between us.

I watch as Heath turns and walks back into the building. I thought coming to an agreement would be easy—the best thing for everyone—but it feels like my heart just took on another bruise.

Standing, I walk back to the Coffee Loft where I'd left my car. Peeking through the window, I see Ashlan is busy with a line of customers, so I decide to go to Anne's. Even if she's busy today, I can sit in an empty salon chair and make small talk.

I pull behind Master Cuts and park next to Anne's pink VW Bug. She put eyelashes on it recently, claiming that the looks she got driving around town were totally worth the forty dollars she spent. She's unique and not afraid to be herself. It's one of the things I love about her. I've grown closer to her since she came back to Piney Brook and took over the salon. She was one of the more popular girls in high school who had big dreams of leaving Piney Brook, whereas I couldn't imagine leaving.

I walk around to the front of the salon and open the door. A jingling bell announces my arrival, and Anne turns to the front door with a comb in her hand. "Be right with . . . Oh! Gabby, hey girl. I didn't expect to see you back so soon."

I smile at Mrs. Govney, who's currently sitting in Anne's chair. "Mind if I sit and watch a while?"

Mrs. Govney, a former high school History teacher, just turns back in her seat. "Suit yourself, dear."

She always has been a grouchy one.

"Have a seat," Anne says, using the comb to point to the empty salon chair beside her. "Mrs. Govney is my last client for the morning. Then I was going to head to Daisy's for lunch. Want to join me?"

I sit in the chair, careful to hold one foot in place so I don't spin in a circle and fall flat on my bottom. "Sure, that'd be great."

I glance at Mrs. Govney and try not to laugh. In high school, the kids called her Elvira behind her back because she always had big hair and lots of makeup, including her signature red lipstick. Not much has changed.

"When I was your age," Mrs. G starts. "I was married and working a real job. When are you going to make your grandma proud and stop waiting tables at that diner?"

My face flushes, and my throat tightens. "I like what I do," I say, holding back tears. Gram had always said to follow my heart. That there was nothing wrong with doing what you enjoy. I'd never really considered doing anything else. I make enough at Beats and Eats to pay the bills, and Gram's house was paid off when she left it to me. Taxes aren't terrible. "I suppose if I change my mind, I'll find something else to do."

Mrs. Govney huffs.

"You're all set to sit under the dryer now," Anne says, closing the last curler. "I'll help you get situated. Would you like some water?" She winks at me and smiles.

"Yes, please," Mrs. G. says. "That dryer makes me parched."

Anne nods. "Right this way."

A few minutes later, Mrs. Govney is under the dryer with her glass of water, and Anne is cleaning up her station.

"Sorry to interrupt," I say, grabbing a broom and sweeping the little bits of hair from her station.

"You're fine. Mrs. Govney's just . . . well, Mrs. Govney. Old stickler won't even let me call her by her first name, and I've been doing her hair for months."

My eyes go wide. "I didn't even know she had a first name," I whisper.

Anne laughs. "She does. It's Gertrude."

I slap my hand over my mouth in an effort not to laugh. "Gertrude Govney?" I ask quietly. No wonder she's grumpy.

"I know, right! Apparently, it's a family name." Anne grins. "I tried calling her Gertie one time. She called my aunt and threatened to never come to Master Cuts again."

"Oh my."

Twenty minutes later, Mrs. G's hair is to her liking, and we are headed to the diner for some lunch. I sit in the passenger seat of Anne's ridiculous car. She's got fluffy pink seat covers with big red lips all over them, a dancing flower attached to the dash, and the eyelashes that flutter in the wind. It's a spectacle, and she seems right at home.

"I'm starving," she says, pulling the car into the parking lot.

"Me too," I say, realizing how true that is.

Once we are seated at a table, and have given Patty our order, Anne clasps her hands together on the table in front of her. "So, what's up?"

"Nothing, just had the morning off and decided to stop in and see how you were doing."

She takes a sip of the coke that Patty dropped off. "Okay. We covered that yesterday. Not much has changed on my end," she says, waiting me out.

"So, are you going to give out candy at Halloween?" I ask, hoping to move the conversation to a more comfortable topic than the one I'm determined to avoid.

She shakes her head. "Not many trick or treaters come to my apartment. I usually skip it and eat pizza and watch scary movies instead. Why are you asking me about Halloween? That's more than a month away."

"It was one of Gram's favorite holidays. She loved passing out candy and seeing all the kids dressed up." I sigh. "I guess I'm just missing her. I could really use her advice these days."

Patty stops at the table, a tray with our food balanced perfectly on her arm. "A club sandwich, fries, and a side of ranch," she says, handing me my order. "And a BLT with a side of onion rings." She puts Anne's plate in front of her. "Don't look now," she whispers, "but there's a trio of brothers that just walked in." She fans herself with her free hand. "I don't think they're from around here. I haven't seen them before," she says with a wink. "I'd for sure remember *them*."

Anne chews her bite of food and looks over her shoulder to where Patty had motioned with her head. She spins back around, fanning her flushed face. "Oh my," she says, taking a sip of her pop.

"Told ya," Patty says, bumping her hip against the table before walking over to the trio of men and taking out her order pad.

"They do look like brothers, triplets maybe," I say while dipping a fry in ranch dressing. They're handsome in that city boy kind of way, but I don't feel a spark.

"I wonder what they're doing in town." Anne says, glancing back over her shoulder.

I shrug. "Who knows."

We finish off our lunch, taking turns guessing where the guys are from and what they're doing in Piney Brook. Anne looks at her watch. "Sorry, I've got to get back."

"No problem, it's almost time to get ready for my shift, anyway."

We pay the bill, and I tell Patty I'll be back in a bit to relieve her. I glance one more time over my shoulder at the men, hoping for a spark of interest. Something to make me believe I have moved on from Heath.

Heath's mom rented the multipurpose room at the church for his party. I glance at the time on my phone before stepping out of the car and smoothing down my dress. Thank goodness we don't get cold weather until the end of October. I can still wear the cute dress with the butterfly sleeves I got last summer. Today

I decided to wear a pair of gold sandals, not the most comfortable shoes I own, but they look great with this sundress. Not that I'm trying to impress anyone. That would be silly. This just happens to be the most comfortable outfit I could find.

I nod my head firmly to reinforce that thought before opening the back door and grabbing the gift bag I brought. Nothing special. The aftershave Heath used to like, a book I thought he might enjoy, and a gift card to the Coffee Loft. Totally friendly gift.

Shutting the door, I take a deep breath to calm my nerves and head for the entryway. The guests are all supposed to be arriving now, and Rosie will bring Heath in about thirty minutes.

I step inside the room and look around. Orange and green streamers dangle from the ceiling along the walls. A "Happy Birthday" sign is pinned up above six-foot tables that have been pushed together to hold cake and finger foods. There's a smaller round table with a bucket of ice, cups, sweet tea and lemonade off to the side. I glance around and spot the gift table. I head there first and drop off the gift bag before beelining it to the sweet tea.

I grab a cup, and write my name on it with a sharpie before adding ice and filling her up with the sweetest sweet tea this side of the Mississippi. Ms. Daisy made up gallons of the stuff, just for today. I turn to step back from the table and spot *them*. Olivia and Zade. They are standing with a tall man, definitely military. Zade is pulling on his mom's arm and pointing to the lemonade.

I move quickly away from the table. I may be starting to believe Zade's not his, and he was just helping out a friend, but I can't help the sting of jealousy that passes through my heart. He'd given us up to protect her. I can't blame him. Not really. After his dad abandoned them, Heath developed a bit of a helper complex. He was always the one to step in for his mom, and others in the community. It's one of the things I love about him. No—*loved*. Past tense.

"Hey! Fancy seeing you here," Evan says, guiding Karlee over to stand by me. "I figured you would be working."

I smile and step into Karlee's hug. She's a hugger, that one. "Nope. I have the weekend off."

"Great! You should totally come with us to Daniel and Reese's after this. They are having a bonfire tonight," Karlee says. "I've been looking forward to it all week." She leans into Evan and he drops a kiss on the top of her head.

"I couldn't impose." I know Daniel and Reese. It's a small town. Not many people I don't know, but I wouldn't say we are friends. Not really. I tend to keep to myself. My small group of people is all I need.

"You wouldn't be," Evan says. "It's a casual thing. The kids will roast s'mores. The more adults for that the merrier. You wouldn't believe how messy kids can get with those things."

I laugh. "I remember them being pretty messy. I'll think about it, okay?" Not really, I've thought about it. I'll be going home, taking a bath, and getting lost in the latest cozy mystery I picked up at the grocery store this week.

"Sure," Evan says, pulling out his phone. "They just got here. Come on, let's get closer to the doors."

I follow behind Karlee and Evan. The group is whispering a countdown, someone trying to coordinate the "Surprise" yell.

The doors open, Heath walks in, and everyone shouts. Zade launches himself into Heath's arms. Heath catches him and swings him around. The pure joy on his face as he brings Zade back down the floor and hugs Olivia makes the back of my eyes sting. Deciding I can't do this after all, I slip quietly behind the crowd and out the side door to the parking lot.

It's clear he loves them. So much that he would pretend to be her baby's father. So much that he would let things end with us. He could have come home on leave and told me before now. He could have said he wanted to be more than friends when I suggested it yesterday.

I'm not enough. I was never enough. Not for my mom, and not for Heath.

CHAPTER NINE

Heath

I knew Mom was up to something when she suggested she drive. She never wants to drive. When we pulled into the church parking lot, she claimed she just needed to pick up some yarn that had been donated for her hats. I offered to wait in the car to call her bluff, but she insisted I come in and help carry the box.

"Okay, but after this, you're letting me treat you to dinner, right?" I ask.

"Sure, of course," she says nervously. "Do you mind getting the door? It's a bit sticky."

I reach out and pull the door open a bit too hard. It definitely wasn't sticky. I laugh when I glance inside and everyone yells "Surprise." Zade is in the front row and launches himself at me like a flying squirrel. I catch him and swing him around before putting him down and leaning in to give Olivia a hug. "You didn't have to come all the way to Piney Brook," I tell her.

Dominic shakes my hand. "Of course we did, you're family."

I don't know why his words choke me up, but they do. I look around and spot Hudson in the corner talking to Anne. Of course, he's already chatting up the single ladies. Or at least, I think she's single.

I make my way around the room, mingling with all the people who took the time out of their day to come to a party for me. I'm a little disappointed that I don't see Gabby. Maybe she's working. Finally, I make my way to Evan.

"Happy birthday, Heath," he says. "Looks like Rosie's still got the party planning touch, huh?"

I laugh. When we were kids, Mom went out of her way to make sure I had the best birthday parties. Everyone in my class got invited, and we'd spend hours playing Nerf guns, or building Legos. One time, she rented a big bounce house. That was endless hours of fun. "I guess so."

"Are you coming to Reese and Daniel's later?" Karlee asks.

"Yeah, I thought I'd stop by." Since I've been home, and spending more time with Evan and Karlee, Brant, and Daniel, and their girls, Morgan and Reese have become part of my circle, too.

"Great!" Karlee says brightly. "I invited Gabby, too." She looks around the room and frowns. "Though I don't see her now. Maybe she stepped into the bathroom."

I look around again.

She came?

How did I miss her?

My heart pounds in my chest. She came.

"I'm sure she'll turn up," I say casually. Hoping not to seem too eager to see her.

"I'm sure," Evan says, giving me a knowing look.

"Uncle Heath," Zade calls. "Is it time for cake?" I laugh. Oh, to be a kid again. The cake was always the highlight of a birthday party.

"You bet!" I say, making my way to the cake table. "Help me blow out the candles?"

Zade grins. "I bet you're gonna need lotsa help. Twenty-five candles is so many!"

I laugh and ruffle his hair before picking him up and holding him on my hip while Mom lights the candles.

"On the count of three," she says as she lights the last one. "One, two, three . . ."

A chorus of the "Happy Birthday" song rings out, and Zade grabs my face and plants a kiss right on my cheek. I hug him tight. "Ready?" I whisper when everyone's done singing.

"Did you make a wish?" Mom asks.

I pause. "I'm too old for that, Ma."

She shakes her head and puts her hands on her hips. "Absolutely not. It's tradition."

"Okay," I say, closing my eyes. *I wish Gabby would give me a second chance.* "Done," I say out loud. "Now, help me blow out these candles and get my wish," I say to Zade, leaning us both down toward the flames, careful to keep him from getting burned.

We blow the candles out in one swoop, and Mom steps in to start cutting the cake.

"What did you wish for, Uncle Heath?" Zade asks.

"He can't tell you that," Olivia says, taking him from my arms. "Then the wish won't come true."

Zade nods sagely. "Yeah, I wished for my diabetes to be better, but I told. That must be why I'm still sick."

My eyes flick to Olivia's. She smiles and kisses his cheek. "The doctor says you're doing great with your insulin pump."

He nods. "Yeah, but I still can't have treats all the time."

Dominic pats his back. "Lots of people have diabetes, Zade. It doesn't stop them from doing amazing things."

I make a mental note to check in with them about Zade's health more often. Since I've been home, it's been easy to take his health for granted. I remember when he was first diagnosed. Scared Olivia and me to death. Finally got Dominic to step in and embrace his role. Thank goodness. I'm not sure what I would have done if Olivia didn't have him. It would have made coming home so much harder.

After finishing the cake, people start to say their goodbyes and leave. Zade rubs his eyes, and his dad scoops him up. "It's about time we got going," he says. "We're going to try to drive back while he sleeps."

I nod. "I appreciate you coming all this way for a few hours."

"We wouldn't miss it," Olivia says, giving me a hug. "Are you and Momma A coming out for Thanksgiving?"

I nod. "I think so. I have to clear it with work and her doctor, but that's the plan for now."

"Just let us know," Dominic says. "You're always welcome."

After walking them to their car and saying goodbye, I step back inside and find my mom. "Thank you for all of this," I say.

"My pleasure." She smiles and pats my hand. "I hoped Gabby would come. She said she would."

"Evan and Karlee said they saw her," I say, frowning. "I never did, though."

"Well, let's get cleaned up so you can go hang out with your friends later."

Karlee did say she'd invited Gabby to the bonfire. Maybe I'll get to see her tonight after all.

I help Mom load the presents into the car, vowing to open them tomorrow when I have more time. I still can't believe anyone got me anything. It's a little weird, if I'm being honest. In the Army, my birthday was just another day. The guys and I maybe went out and grabbed a burger, but we didn't make it a big deal. I'm out of practice with these things.

Turns out, Gabby skipped the bonfire last night. I don't know why I thought she might be there. I stayed out later than I had planned in case she decided to stop by after all. I want to ask her why she left the party before I was able to see her. Friends can ask that, right?

I should have asked her if she'll answer my calls or texts now that we are friends.

After taking a shower and getting dressed, I head down the hall and into the kitchen to make myself some breakfast. I've just plated my eggs when mom comes in. "Can I make you some?" I ask.

"No, thanks. I already had my avocado toast." She sits at the table and watches as I put butter and jam on mine. "How was last night?"

"It was good. It was nice hanging out with everyone. Even though being the only single one feels weird sometimes." I take my plate and join her at the table.

"After breakfast, do you want to open your presents?"

I finish chewing my eggs before answering. "Yeah, I told Zade I'd open his first and video call so he can watch."

Mom smiles. "He's such a good kid. I see Dominic and Olivia are getting along well. I'm so happy for them."

"Me too," I say, pushing my plate away. "They deserve a happy family."

Mom's grin falters.

"Not that you didn't deserve that, too," I say.

"No, I know," she says, reaching over to pat my hand. "Sometimes things don't turn out the way we hope."

"Did you ever think of moving on?" I ask. Mom never dated after Dad left. She used to say she had me and that was enough. As a little kid, that felt like a good answer. Now, I'm not so sure.

"I'm happy with how things are," she says, looking away. "When your father left, I was so broken. I didn't think my heart would ever heal. I poured myself into work, and raising you the best way I knew how."

I stand and hug her tight. "You did a great job, Ma. If you want to find love again, I'd support that."

She shakes her head. "I'm in my fifties now, Heath. My time has passed. I look forward to the day you start your own family."

Now it's my turn to look away. *How can I start a family of my own when the only woman I could see as my wife just wants to be friends?* "Let's go open some presents."

Mom follows me into the living room and slides into her rocking chair, flipping the lever to lift her feet. "I'll hold the phone," she says when I dial Olivia's number.

"Hello?" Olivia answers.

"You look tired," I say. She's got bags under her eyes and looks like she didn't sleep a wink all night.

"It's not easy to sleep in a car, and I've stayed up so that Zade didn't miss your call this morning."

"Well, I'll make this quick so you can go rest. Can I see my best buddy?"

Olivia hands the phone to Zade. "Hey, dude," I say when his big grin is on the screen. "Pull the phone back a bit, remember?"

Zade laughs. "Oh, yeah. Are you opening my present now?"

I hold it up so he can see. "I'm giving the phone to Grandma Rosie so she can hold it while I unwrap, okay?"

He nods and squirms in his seat. "Hurry up!"

Laughing, I hand the phone to Mom and wait for her to nod. "Here we go," I say, dramatically tearing the paper off the package. I open the box and pull out the shirt inside. It's got a picture of Zade and me from the zoo and says "Best Uncle Ever." "Wow, Zade!" I choke back tears. "It's perfect!"

"Are you going to wear it today?" he asks excitedly.

"Of course," I say, taking my t-shirt off and replacing it with his gift.

He grins and pulls his blanket off showing me his matching shirt. Except his says "Best Nephew Ever." "Now we match!"

I grin. "That's perfect," I say. "Next time we go to the zoo, we'll have to wear these shirts so everyone knows how awesome we are. What do you say?"

"Yeah!" He looks to his right where I'm sure Olivia is beside him on the couch. "Mommy said it's time to go so she can take a nap."

I nod my head. "Sounds good to me. Be good so your mom and dad can sleep some today, okay?"

"I will. Bye, Uncle Heath."

"Bye, little man."

He hits the end button, and the call cuts off.

"That was so sweet," Mom says, wiping at her eyes with the corner of her shirt.

"It was." I reach for another present. A gift bag this time. "I wonder who this one's from. I don't see a tag." I reach inside the bag and pull out a book. A thriller, just like I used to read. Next, I pull out a bottle of aftershave, my favorite kind. I reach into the bag again and swirl my hand around, looking for a card. Feeling something, I grab it and pull it out. A gift card to the Coffee Loft.

"No card?" Mom asks.

"No," I say, looking at the items again. "But I have a good idea who it's from. Do you mind if we open the rest later? I have an errand to run."

CHAPTER TEN

Gabby

It's Sunday morning, which means the diner doesn't open until eleven. I usually try to make it to church, but today I just didn't feel like making the effort. I'm in my pajamas, my hair in a messy bun, drinking coffee from a mug I bought from the Coffee Loft this summer that says "Sip, Read, Repeat" with a stack of books. I grab my cozy mystery from the coffee table and scoot back onto the couch. May as well get lost in the story for a while.

I'm just to the good part, when there's a knock at the door. What in the world? I slide my bookmark back in place—because, really, who dog-ears a book?—and set it back down next to my cold coffee. That'll have to go back into the microwave.

There's another knock at the door. "Coming," I call. Hopefully, Mrs. Johnston didn't lose her cat again. I don't really want to spend the next hour walking around the house calling for Ms. Prittens. I swing the door open, ready to tell Mrs. Johnston I can't help, when my mouth falls open and I squeak. I actually squeak.

"Can I come in?" Heath's big brown eyes take in my pajamas and crazy hair. "Or is this a bad time?"

I close my mouth. At this point, he's seen me in all my fleece-pajama glory. What difference does it make? We're friends, right? That word feels like sandpaper in my brain.

"Sure," I step back and motion for him to come inside. "I was just taking it easy before I go into work in a little bit."

He nods and stuffs his hands in his pockets. "Thanks for the gifts."

I feel my face heat. He knows it was from me? "You're welcome. I think I forgot to put a card in it." More like "didn't put my name on it in case I needed to flee."

"Yeah, I noticed." His eyes roam my face. "Why didn't you stay?"

I consider making up an excuse, but the pain in his eyes stops me. "I was overwhelmed," I say. It's the truth. "I saw you with Olivia and Zade, and . . . I don't know. It was too much."

He shakes his head. "I'm sorry. I'm so sorry. If I could go back and make sure you knew the truth before that day, I would."

"I believe you," I whisper.

"I never loved her. Not like you're thinking. She's a friend. She needed help. I couldn't turn her away. You know that."

I nod, tears sliding down my cheeks. "I know. It just hurts to see them with you because it brings back the pain from being dumped." There, I said it.

He opens his mouth to argue and then closes it again. "I'm so sorry. It never should have happened. I shouldn't have broken up with you. I thought I was doing you a favor by freeing you. We were so young, and I didn't want you to put your life on hold for me."

I swipe the tears from my cheeks. "We can't change the past, Heath. All we can do is move forward."

He reaches out and takes my hand. "I'd like to be friends again, but I'm going to tell you now, Gabby. I want more. I want it all. I wish I'd asked you to marry me that summer."

My eyes snap to his. "You *what?*"

"I know we were young. We thought we had plenty of time, but I knew then that I wanted you forever."

I shake my head. "No, we were kids. You couldn't have known that," I argue, but a voice in my head stops me. *Didn't you know?*

I did.

I knew the day he left that my heart had gone with him.

"I did," he insists. "I didn't feel like I was good enough for you yet. Felt like I had to prove I could handle being a man, learn some skills to take care of you, of a family, before I asked you. So when you asked if we could keep it a secret from everyone, I agreed. I was stupid."

"You weren't stupid, Heath. You were young, barely an adult when you left." I pull my hand from his and walk over to the couch, sitting down. "Things have a way of working out the way they are supposed to. Maybe we weren't supposed to be together forever."

He shakes his head. "I disagree. I want to prove to you that we still have that spark. That we still belong together, and if you don't feel the same way . . . well, I'll settle for being friends. Not having you in my life these past few years has been painful, Gabby." He sits down on the opposite end of the couch. "So, I'd like to start by being friends. Real friends, not friendly acquaintances or whatever you called it the other day. I want to get to know the Gabby you are now."

I take a minute to think about what he's saying. "Friends."

He nods.

"I can do that."

"Great," he says, pulling out his phone. "I don't know if you got a new number, but mine is the same."

I shake my head. "No, I have the same number."

He looks at me, puzzled. "Then why didn't you ever answer when I called or texted?"

I take a deep breath. "You broke my heart. I blocked your number."

He nods. "Will you unblock me now?"

I stand and head to my room. Taking my phone off the charger, I open the contacts as I walk back into the living room. "Done," I say, putting the phone in my pocket.

"And you'll answer me?"

I hesitate, and he must take that as a no.

"How about we text for a while first? That way, you can answer me when you're ready."

"Okay."

He glances down at his phone, taps the screen a few times, and puts it in his pocket. My phone chimes with an incoming text.

"All right, I'm going to go so you can get ready for work." He walks to the front door. "I'll talk to you later." Then he slips outside, and he's gone.

It's the middle of the after-church rush, and the diner is packed. "Order up," Ricky calls from behind the cook's line.

"Thanks, Ricky," I say, putting the plates on a tray.

"You got it," he says, giving me a thumbs up before grabbing another ticket off the printer. "It's hopping in here today."

I nod. "Need anything?"

He grins. "I wouldn't turn down a cold sweet tea when you get a chance."

"I got it," Patty says from beside me. "You take your food out."

"Thanks," Ricky and I say at the same time.

The rest of the day passes in a blur of faces. "Jeez," Patty says, wiping her last table down. "I don't think we've had a Sunday that busy since I started."

Ms. Daisy walks by with the cash drawer, headed to the office to close out for the day. "It was just like old times, wasn't it, Gabby?"

I smile as I fill the sugar containers on the counter in front of me. "Yes, it was."

I finish my side work and help Patty with hers. "How'd you do?" she asks.

"I haven't counted, but judging from how full my pocket is, I'd say I may have added enough to savings to get the garage door fixed."

She giggles. "Any more trash-tastrophies?"

"No, thankfully. I've managed to keep the critters from knocking the cans over by duct taping the lids down."

Ricky must overhear me from the kitchen because he busts out laughing. "You taped the lids onto your trash cans? I bet the trash guys love that."

Patty's giggles turn into a full belly laugh.

"What's so funny?" Ms. Daisy asks, walking back to the front of the store.

"Gabby's garage door isn't working, and she's taping the lids of her trash cans down to keep the critters out," Patty says between laughs.

Ms. Daisy chuckles. "You should ask Heath to take a look for you. He's always been handy with stuff like that." Ms. Daisy shoots me a pointed look.

"I couldn't," I argue. "He's busy enough with work and his mom. He doesn't need to be worried about me, too."

Ms. Daisy shakes her head. "If you don't believe that boy worries about you day and night, you're not as smart as I thought, young lady."

Patty stops laughing and looks between Ms. Daisy and me like she's watching a pickleball tournament. "Is that why he always sits where he can see you?" she asks. "I wondered if there was something there."

"Nope," I say, grabbing my purse off the counter. "Just friends."

"Mm-hmm." Ms. Daisy shakes her head. "And my apple pie is just *okay*."

Needing to escape before this becomes any more awkward, I head to the front doors. "I'll see you tomorrow."

I push my way outside and head for the car. I turn my cell phone back on and wait for it to boot up. After I got another text from Heath at work today, I chickened out and turned the whole phone off. When the phone finishes doing its thing, I see I have three missed texts and a missed call.

I open the call history first. Spam. Of course.

Then I switch to the text app. Three messages. All from Heath.

Heath: Thank you for unblocking me.

That was the one he sent before leaving my house this morning.

Heath: I've started the book. You always did pick the best books.

My heart flutters. He started the book? Already? Something about that feels intimate. Books are my love language. After Heath and I broke up, I stopped reading romance and switched to Fantasy and Cozy Mystery. My heart couldn't take someone else getting their "happily ever after" when mine had gone up in flames.

Heath: Would you like to go to the Fall Festival with me next month? As friends?

I put the phone back into my purse. I can't sit in the parking lot all night staring at my phone. That would be weird. I pull out of the lot just as Ricky, Ms. Daisy, and Patty step out of the diner.

I pull into my driveway and groan. The trash bandits have struck again. Maybe asking Heath for help wouldn't be such a bad idea. Especially since I've been saving up and can pay him.

I spend the next thirty minutes picking up and rebagging the trash from the yard. I don't bother taping the lids. Apparently, the little buggers have figured out how to outmaneuver me.

Once the yard is clean, I head inside for a hot shower. *What a day.* I remember Heath's texts while I'm getting into my pajamas. I head to the kitchen and make myself a snack of milk and cookies before grabbing my phone and settling onto the couch.

Gabby: I'm glad you like the book. I wasn't sure if you still read thrillers.

There, I responded. Setting the phone down, I dunk a cookie into the milk and count to five. Any longer, and the cookie breaks, but any sooner, and it's still crunchy. Tonight calls for soggy cookies.

My phone dings with an incoming text. I swipe it open.

Heath: I haven't had a lot of time to read lately, but I'm happy to say I do still like thrillers.

Not sure what else to say, I set the phone down on the arm rest and dunk another cookie.

Heath: Did you want to think about the Fall Festival?

The cookie I'm eating goes down the wrong way and I sputter. When I'm sure I'm not going to choke to death, I take a sip of the milk to soothe my now-raw throat.

Gabby: I don't know. Just the two of us feels like too much pressure.

Now I wait. I can't risk being more than friends with him. No matter how much I want to. I can't take getting hurt again. Going to the festival, even as friends, feels too much like a date.

Heath: Noted. I understand. Goodnight, Gabby.

I dunk another cookie. Being *just* friends is turning out to be harder than I expected.

CHAPTER ELEVEN

Heath

The following week passes quickly. Every morning I send Gabby a "good morning" text, and I ask her about her day each evening. She's slowly opening up, though she still hasn't agreed to go to the festival with me.

"It's Friday, Heath. What are you still doing here?" Bradley asks.

"Sorry, boss. Just finishing up taping this room." And I lost track of time daydreaming about Gabby.

"How much longer? I'm ready to cut out of here."

I glance around the room. "I can clean up and finish Monday."

Bradley nods. "Need help?"

"Nah. Thanks, though." I pack up all the tools, closing the putty containers and making sure the mess is at least contained before heading to the front. "This job's about over. Any idea what's coming next?"

Bradley grins. "Eager to move onto the next job site?"

I shrug. "Just curious. I want to know what our schedule looks like around Thanksgiving."

"Ah," Bradley nods. "Right. Well, we take Thanksgiving week off entirely. No sense in making the crew come in for a day or two when they could be spending time with family, especially if they travel."

"Good to know," I say, relieved that it looks like Mom and I can head to Olivia and Dominic's for the holiday.

"We take the week of Christmas through the second of the year off, too. In case you were wondering." Bradley motions for me to leave the building before him.

"Perfect," I say. This job has turned out to have more perks than I expected. Coming home from the Army, I wasn't sure what I'd be able to get for work. Especially in a small town like Piney Brook. Apparently, construction is always in demand, no matter how big the town.

"You have a good weekend," Bradley says as he locks the building. "Don't get into too much trouble." He laughs at his own joke. If anyone would be getting in trouble this weekend, it's Hudson. That man is always up for a good time. Still acts like a kid. Not that he's any younger than I am—we've just lived very different lives.

Once I'm settled in the truck, I take out my phone and text Gabby.

Heath: How was your day, beautiful?

A few minutes later, my phone dings with a text. My fingers itch to check it, but I'm driving, and that's a big no-no. It takes all my concentration to wait until I pull into the driveway before I snatch the phone off the seat beside me and open the screen.

Gabby: Could have been better . . .

I click the attachment she sent. It looks like someone, or something, dumped her trash cans all over her yard.

Heath: Ouch! How'd they get into the cans? I thought Gram always kept them in the garage.

I hop out of the truck and head inside, toeing my work boots off at the front door.

"I'm home," I call out before remembering that Mom was going to the cancer survivor support group tonight.

My phone dings with another notification.

Gabby: Yeah, well. The door sticks and I can't for the life of me get it to open.

I smile. Not because Gabby is having a hard time with her house, but because this is something I can do for her.

Heath: I can fix it for you. Give me thirty minutes to shower, and I'll head that way.

I don't wait for her to tell me no. I rush into my room and grab some clothes that I don't mind getting dirty, but are a step above my work uniform. An old t-shirt from high school with George Strait on it, and a less ratty pair of blue jeans. It will do.

I rush through my shower and get into my clothes in record time. I check my phone, and, sure enough . . . Gabby's trying to refuse my help. Stubborn woman.

Gabby: Oh no, you've worked all day. It can wait.

Heath: I'm on my way. Want to grab pizza after?

I hold my breath. Would she refuse pizza? It's her favorite food. Or it used to be.

I slide my shoes back on while I wait for her answer. I'm stepping out onto the front porch when she sends it.

Gabby: I've got lasagna in the oven. I could share.

I throw my fist in the air in celebration. She's letting me in. At least a little bit.

Heath: Sounds perfect. On my way.

A few minutes later, I'm pulling into the driveway behind Gabby's old Jeep. Memories of driving her home that last summer, holding her hand, hearing her sing along to the country music take me back to a time that seemed so simple. So perfect.

I step out of the truck and head to the garage door to check it out. I'm hoping the seals just need to be replaced. Easy enough. We'll see.

I hear the front door open and turn to see Gabby standing there watching me. "You didn't want to come in and say hello first?" she asks, a smile on her face.

"Figured I'd get right to it. I'm sure you don't want to spend all night with me in your space," I say, secretly wishing she did.

A light blush stains her cheeks. "Maybe not all night," she says before turning and heading through the front door, leaving it open for me to follow.

"It smells amazing in here." The smell of bubbling cheese and marinara sauce hits my nose the moment I step through the door.

"Thanks," she says simply before turning toward the kitchen and the door that leads to the garage. "Want to see it from the inside?"

"You bet," I say, following her lead.

Out in the garage, I can already tell the garage door tracks are dirty. "That could be the problem," I say, pointing to them. "The springs look okay, so unless the tracks are bent somehow, or the rubber seal needs replacing, it should be a fairly easy fix."

Gabby shakes her head. "Seriously? It's *dirty*? It's a garage door. Aren't they always dirty?"

I laugh. "Well, it's not the cleanest place in the house, but I'll get it cleaned up and lubricated. We'll see if that does the trick."

She nods. "Thanks."

"Have you considered putting in an automatic garage door opener?"

"Nope. I don't need it. No sense in spending money on things I don't need."

"Got it," I say, trying to hide my smile. Gabby was always the practical one, where I was quick to jump on the things that would make my life, and the lives of those I cared about, a little easier. "I'll head out to the truck and get my stuff. This shouldn't take too long."

"Need help?" she asks. "I don't mind getting dirty."

I shake my head. "No, ma'am. You're going to go inside and check on that delicious-smelling dinner, then put your feet up and read that book I saw on your coffee table."

"You don't have to tell me twice," she says, grinning. "Thanks, Heath."

"No problem, Gabby. I'll always help you out. You should know that." I walk through the door and out to the truck before she can respond.

I'm in the garage, just finishing wiping down the tracks when Gabby steps out. "Dinner's done, can you take a break?"

I wipe my hands on a clean cloth beside me and take a step back. "Yeah, I've got the tracks cleaned up. After we eat, I'll grease up the rollers and see if we can't get her open."

"You can wash up in the bathroom," Gabby says pointing down the hall. "I'm guessing you remember where it is?"

I nod. "I remember everything about you," I say, softly.

Gabby turns and slides oven mitts on both hands before pulling open the oven door. "Go clean up while I make us plates."

"Yes, ma'am."

Once in the bathroom, I wash my hands and face before giving myself a pep talk. *This is Gabby, your girl. She's letting you in. Don't mess it up.* Well, kind of sad as pep talks go, but, hey . . .

"I hope you're hungry," she calls from the kitchen.

"Starving, actually," I call back. When I step back into the hallway, I see Gabby has plated the food—lasagna, garlic bread, and side salads—and placed everything on the dining table in the corner of the room.

I pull out the chair that used to be hers, and wait for her to sit before taking the spot beside her instead of across from her. I wanted to be close, and she doesn't seem to mind.

"So," I say, picking up my fork. "Besides the trash pandas, how was your week?" I'm dying to know everything about her again.

"It was good. The diner is busy this time of year. Ms. Daisy's thinking of retiring soon. Don't tell anyone."

I raise an eyebrow. Somehow I don't see Ms. Daisy retiring, but I guess she is getting older. "What will she do with the diner?"

Gabby finishes chewing her bite and takes a sip of water. "Well," she starts. "I'm not supposed to say anything, so don't repeat this, okay?"

She's trusting me. I could whoop or pump my fist I'm so excited. "Of course not, Gabby. You can trust me. I promise."

She eyes me for a minute before seemingly deciding she can. "Ms. Daisy has asked if I want to take on the role of manager. She'll still own it, but I'll do all the day-to-day stuff. She'll help me, of course, while I learn, but the diner will be mine to run."

I set my fork on my plate so I can grasp her hands. "That's amazing! You've always loved working in the diner. This will be the next level up for you!"

She smiles before dropping her eyes. "Yeah, but what if Gram would be disappointed? I mean, I've only ever worked at the diner. I never went to school to *be* something, you know?"

"No, I don't know. I didn't really go to school either. I was trained in the Army. I couldn't imagine working a desk job. I need to work somewhere where

I can use my hands and create something. Would you want to be doing anything else?"

"Not really," Gabby says, taking another bite of her food.

"Then I think Gram would be happy for you. She only ever encouraged us to follow our dreams and do what makes us happy. *Our* dreams, Gabby. Not someone else's."

Gabby shakes her head. "Sometimes it feels dangerous to dream," she whispers. "Dreams don't tend to come true."

"Well, this one is. This sounds like the perfect opportunity for you. I'm proud of you, Gabby, and I know Gram would be, too."

A tear slides down her cheek, and it just about guts me right here at the table.

"Dreams do come true. The ones that are meant to, that is." I hope she can sense the sincerity in my voice—the things I'm not quite saying.

CHAPTER TWELVE

Gabby

After dinner, Heath does some magic and the next thing I know, the garage door is sliding up and down like it's brand new. "Thank you," I say, as I drag in a trash can. Heath has the other one, bringing it in right behind me.

"My pleasure," he says, scooting his can close to mine. "Now you don't have to worry about anything getting into your trash."

He looks so handsome standing there in the George Strait t-shirt he got that summer at a country music festival we went to. Why'd he have to wear something that would bring back so many memories? "Do you remember that summer?" I ask, my mouth moving before my brain has caught up.

"All the time," Heath says softly. "I remember every moment of that summer with you."

I nod. "Me too."

"Gabby," he says, his voice strained. "I want that again."

I suck in a breath. My chest feels like my heart is trying to escape. "But, last time . . . you changed your mind. I don't want to open myself up to that again. I'm scared."

"I know," he says, stepping close and pulling me in for a hug. "I was a kid. I thought I was doing the right thing by letting you out of our deal. I was dumb. Ever since then, I've held onto hope. I know it's been a long time, but I hope we can be close again someday." The smell of the aftershave I got him for his birthday fills my nose, bringing those memories closer to the surface. "That's why I want to get to know you again. Take this slowly. I want to prove to you that I'm worth taking the risk."

My head falls to his chest. "Thank you," I whisper.

"I'll always put you first."

But he didn't. That thought has me stepping out of his arms. "Thank you for fixing the door," I say, wrapping my arms around my middle.

He must sense the change in me because he nods and grabs his tools. "You're welcome. I should get back home. See if Mom made it home from her support group yet."

I nod and watch him walk to his truck and slide inside. For a moment I let myself remember, let myself feel. I only hope that doesn't come back to bite me.

Lacey and I agree to meet for lunch at a nearby barbecue restaurant, and I am glad Knox is off and can keep Matti so Lacey can come alone. I've been so conflicted since Heath came and fixed the door. I could use some time with my bestie to take my mind off of it all.

After we place our order, we find a booth in the back of the small dining area and slide in.

"I'm so glad you agreed to come to lunch," Lacey says. "It's almost like you've been avoiding me."

I roll my eyes. "Why on earth would I avoid you? You're my best friend, silly."

"Maybe because you've been spending more time with a certain someone," she says. "Having a boyfriend takes up more of your free time." She would know. Since she and Knox got together, and the build-out for the center has been underway she's been busier than ever.

I sigh. "I see the rumor mill has been working overtime lately."

She leans forward and shrugs her shoulders. "I think everyone is waiting for you and Heath to stop pretending like you're just friends."

I scoff. "Seriously? We *are* just friends." Even if these last few weeks of texting back and forth have been making me want more. Making me wish for things that have long since passed.

"Yep," she says, sitting back for the waiter to place our food on the table. "You keep telling yourself that."

I try to contain the blush that I can feel racing across my cheeks, and fail. "Whatever. This food looks delicious." I grab my fork and knife and dig into the brisket with more force than necessary. It's a good thing she's my best friend, or I'd leave right now. Okay, so running away from my problems isn't mature, but it beats getting hurt. An ache takes up residence in my stomach, and a little voice niggles in my head. *Why are you still hurting even with Heath locked in the friend zone?*

Nope. Not going there.

"I'm not going to ask you about Heath anymore. I know there's more to the story than what you've told me so far. Otherwise, you wouldn't be so guarded," Lacey says after a few minutes of awkward silence.

I open my mouth to argue.

"I just want you to know that I'm here for you, and when you're ready to share, I'm ready to listen," Lacey says, holding her hand up to stop me. She glances at her sticky fingertips and draws each of them into her mouth, sucking off the lingering sauce.

I search my mind for something to say, but come up short. "Okay," I finally say with a nod.

The rest of the lunch is filled with talk about the progress with the center, and while I couldn't be happier for my friend, I can't get my mind off of Heath.

The next day, the diner is slow and Ms. Daisy has me in her office going over purchase orders. "Are you sure I can handle this?" I ask, taking in all of the paperwork in front of me.

"Of course you can." Ms. Daisy pats my hand. "You've worked here for years. I'd venture to say if anyone knows this place as well as I do, it would be you."

I nod. "But that doesn't mean I'm ready to take over the management tasks." I point to the inventory sheet. "That I've done, but this . . ." I say waving my hand at the computer and the program Ms. Daisy uses to do each week's ordering. "What if I mess up and order too much, or too little?"

Ms. Daisy laughs. "Girl, you know as well as I do that if you have too much, you put it on special. Too little, you just tell them it was our most popular dish and they'll need to come in earlier next week." She winks. "Seriously, Gabby. I wouldn't have asked if I didn't think you could do it."

I summon all my courage and smile. "I know. Thank you."

"Now, let's see what we need."

An hour later, I think I finally understand how to place the weekly order. If only I felt confident that I wouldn't mess it up and cost the diner—and Ms. Daisy—money, I'd feel better. Money was always tight for me and Gram. She hadn't expected to have to raise her granddaughter in her retirement years, but we managed. I struggle to hold back the tears that burn the backs of my eyelids. *You can cry later, Gabby. Right now, you have work to do.*

"You are welcome to go home for the day," Ms. Daisy says. "I don't think we're going to get a rush until this evening, and I've got that covered."

"You sure?" I ask.

Ms. Daisy nods. "Yes, ma'am. Go on, get out of here and do something fun while the weather is still warm enough." She winks and shoos me out of the office.

"I'll see you tomorrow," I say, grabbing my things and making a quick getaway.

As I walk to the car, I'm hit with a sudden longing to go to the lakeshore. There's a spot I haven't been to since that summer when I was last there with Heath. I look up at the gray sky and decide to go now. What's a Monday afternoon off if I don't do something for myself?

An hour later, I'm parked in the lot that leads to the sandy beach of the lake. I slide my sandals off, tossing them onto the floorboard. "Just a walk along the shore," I say out loud to myself, grabbing my towel and shutting the Jeep door.

As my feet hit the warm sand, I sigh. I let the rough, wet sand slide between my toes, grounding me in a way that I only feel here. Setting off near the lapping water, I am careful not to get too wet. I didn't bring my suit, I just wanted to think.

My mind takes me back to the last time I was here with Heath. We laughed and kicked up the water like a couple of kids. I guess we *were kids*. I smile at the memory. Both of us, covered in sand and water, laughing and splashing without a care in the world.

I miss that version of myself. The one that thought true love might actually exist. That not everyone you love hurts you. I knew Heath would be leaving for the Army, but it was only a few years. I could do anything for the man I loved. Or so I thought.

I wonder again what would have happened if I'd accepted the truth about Olivia back then. Could I have accepted our new "just friends" status as well? Would it have bothered me that he was playing house with her while those around him thought he'd cheated on me?

Stopping to look out over the water and watch the birds swooping and diving after their meals, I realize that, yes, it would have bothered me, but if he had shared it with me and kept our promise, I would have understood. I felt betrayed because his promise to me meant nothing to him. We said forever, and he said nine months was enough. He decided. I didn't get a say.

He'd hurt me, and while I can forgive him—even understand it to a point. I just can't risk opening my heart again. And I'm okay being alone. Gram was alone after Pops died when I was a baby. She was happy. *Wasn't she?*

I move back to a soft, dry part of the shore and put out my towel, then drop down to take a seat and stretch out my legs. I should have come here sooner. I forgot how much I love sitting and listening to the lake sounds. Boats out on the water, their engines whirring, birds calling to each other, an occasional frog croaking, people laughing and enjoying themselves. It's peaceful today since it's during the week, allowing my thoughts the quiet they need to wander.

"Gabby?"

Startled at the sound of my name, I let out a yelp.

"Sorry!" Heath says, holding up his hands. "I didn't mean to scare you."

Heath. Is here. At the lake.

"It's okay," I say, my hand over my racing heart. "I didn't realize I wasn't alone anymore."

Heath nods. "I see that." He points to the ground beside me. "Mind if I sit?" *Do I?* "Of course not," I say.

He takes his time, settling down onto the sand near enough I can smell his cologne. I close my eyes.

"I didn't expect to see you here," he says, placing his arms around his knees.

"I came on a whim. The diner was slow today, so I was off early." I don't mention it's my first time back in years. That would be too weird.

"I've missed this place," he says after a few moments of silence.

"Me too," I say. "I don't have much time to get out here." There, that explains why I would miss it, right?

He nods and looks back out at the water. "Kentucky was a beautiful place to be stationed, but there's nothing quite like home, you know?"

"Not really," I say, truthfully. "I haven't really gone anywhere to be able to compare."

He glances at me. "Really? You haven't traveled at all in the last few years?"

"Nope," I say.

"What happened? You always wanted to go see the jungle and climb volcanoes."

"I didn't feel like it. After Gram died, I had the house to take care of, which took time and money. Then I had some *things* happen that took the wind out of me." I look at him and he gives me a tight-lipped nod to show he understands. "So, I decided to stay where I know how life is supposed to work."

We both stare out at the water. The silence should feel awkward, but it feels . . . nice.

"What about you? What brings you out here today?"

He looks out over the water and takes a deep breath. "I took the day off to do some things around the house for Mom. I finished earlier than I expected and had the urge to come out here. It's one of my favorite spots."

I smile. "Mine too."

"Do you think we could ever get back there? To the carefree teenagers in love?"

The vulnerability in his gaze pops the stitches on my newly mended heart. "I don't think so," I whisper. "Times have changed. We've changed. I don't think I'd want to go back to those naive kids, even if we could."

"I still love you," he says softly, taking my hand in his.

Tears fill my eyes. "I've got to go." I pull my hand from his and start the trek back to the car. The tears that I've been holding back start to fall when I catch sight of the Jeep. On the windshield, under my wiper, is a bunch of wildflowers.

He always knew how to reach my heart.

CHAPTER THIRTEEN

Heath

I stare out at the water for a long time after Gabby leaves. I was surprised when I saw her car in the lot. What are the odds of us both coming here today?

It seemed like fate was finally on my side.

Until I opened my big mouth.

Of course I had to go and ask for more than she's ready to give.

If I wasn't certain she still loved me too, I'd give up. But I don't think I could move on. She's it for me. I knew it when I was eighteen, and it hasn't changed in all these years. Being back home, so close to her, only makes me want it more. I can't believe that she doesn't still feel something. A love like ours doesn't just disappear, does it?

My phone rings, and I pull it from my pocket. Mom's face pops up on the screen. Swiping, I answer it. "Hello?"

"Heath," Mom says, sounding winded. "Do you think you can come home? Something's not quite right."

I take off at a sprint. "I'm on my way. Do you need me to call 911?" Mom hasn't been feeling well the last couple of days, but we both thought it was a cold and would run its course. Now I'm not so sure.

"No," she says, her voice shaky. "I think I'll be okay, but I'd feel better if you were here."

"I'll be there as soon as I can. I'm going to hang up now and call Evan to come over until I can get there, okay?"

She takes a shaky breath. "Okay. Please hurry. But drive safely."

"I will." I hang up the phone and don't stop running until I'm at the truck. Hitting the button to unlock the door, I slide inside, not taking the time to brush the sand from my body. I take a deep breath and pull up Evan's number. It rings twice before he picks up.

"Heath, what's up?"

I lose it. Before I can say anything, I'm sobbing.

"Heath! Hey, man, you're scaring me," Evan says. "What happened? Is it your mom?"

Through choked sobs, I manage to tell him I need him to go to her.

"I'm on my way," Evan says. I can hear the door of his apartment slam shut. "You've got to pull yourself together. She's going to be fine. You can't drive when you're like this, and she needs you."

He stays on the line until I can breathe again. "Thanks, man," I say, putting the truck in reverse and pulling out of the parking space. "I think I panicked."

"You've needed to let all this out for a while. I'm not surprised you lost it for a minute," he says. "I'm pulling into her driveway now."

"Thanks, I'm on my way, but I'm hanging up now so I can drive. Call me if anything happens."

"You got it," Evan says before disconnecting the call.

Thirty-five minutes later, I'm pulling into the driveway behind Evan's truck. I've barely come to a stop before I'm throwing it in park and opening the door. Running up the sidewalk, I push open the front door and stop in my tracks.

"Hey," Evan says, holding Mom's hand. "I'm thinking she may need to go get checked out."

"Now, Evan, I told you I don't need to go to the hospital," Mom says, her voice weak.

"And I told *you* that we'd see what Heath thinks when he gets here." Evan motions with his head to the dining room. "We'll be right back." He pats Mom's hand before letting go.

I follow him. "What?" I ask, unable to get more words out.

"Her breathing seems pretty labored. I'm sure she's fine, but I texted Karlee, and she said she thinks she needs to be assessed. Especially with her history of cancer and chemo."

I nod. "Thanks. I wouldn't have thought to ask Karlee."

He pats my shoulder. "I'm here for you."

We walk back into the living room, and I kneel down by Mom. "Hey," I say, reaching for her hand. Her head is resting back on the couch and her eyes are closed. "Mom?"

Evan curses under his breath and I hear him on the phone with 911.

"Mom!"

It feels like an eternity, but finally, the ambulance shows up and the medics whisk Mom away. They say she's breathing, but not well.

"Let's go," Evan says, grabbing my arm. "We'll follow them to the hospital."

We get outside, and Evan hops into the driver's seat of my truck. "Seriously, dude? Sand?" He glances at me and cringes. "Sorry, not the time." He follows behind the ambulance to Piney Brook General, where they rush Mom inside.

"You'll have to go to the front desk and get her checked in. They'll let you know something as soon as they can," one of the medics says on his way past us.

I nod, but I can't make my feet move.

Evan grabs me by the shoulders and pushes me in the direction of the sliding doors. "This way," he says.

Once we are inside, I give my name and information to the man working the desk. "Have a seat and we'll call you as soon as we can."

I want to argue, but I can't. Evan and I take a seat in the corner and wait.

After what feels like an eternity, a doctor comes through the doors and calls my name.

"Go," Evan says. "I'll wait here."

I nod and make my way to where the doctor is waiting.

"I'm Rosanna Atkins's son, Heath."

He motions for me to follow him through the double doors. "Heath, your mom is currently stable, but she's got pneumonia. Unfortunately, with her chemotherapy and radiation, her lungs are weak."

My heart slams into my ribcage before stopping all together. The doctor must see my panic because he stops and puts his hand on my arm.

"She can pull through this," he says.

Finally, my heart beats again. "I sense a but . . ."

He nods. "We need to transfer her to Little Rock. They have an impeccable pulmonology department and state-of-the-art ICU. She'll be able to get the best care there."

Little Rock. That's three hours away without traffic. "How long will she be there?" I ask.

"I'd expect at least ten days." He motions down the hallway. "Would you like to see her before we transport her? She's awake, but she's weak, and she has an oxygen mask on."

I nod. "Please."

The doctor stops and motions to a partially closed door. "She's in there. You can only stay for a few minutes."

I nod. "Thanks," I say. I step into the sterile hospital room and fight back the tears that want to fall. I'm scared, but I don't want Mom to know. "Hey, Mom," I say, picking up her hand. "You gave me a bit of a scare."

She shakes her head. "I . . ."

"It's okay," I blurt. "Don't use your energy to talk to me now, but we'll be discussing your practical jokes later, okay?"

She nods.

"They're going to move you to the hospital in Little Rock."

She nods again.

"I'll be right behind you, okay? I'm just going to get some clothes from the house, and I'll be on my way."

She shakes her head.

"No arguing." I pat her hand. "You'd do the same for me." I lean in and give her a kiss on the forehead. She closes her eyes and sighs.

"She needs her rest," a nurse says, stepping into the room.

"I'll see you soon," I say, placing another kiss on her cheek.

Stepping into the hallway, I take a deep breath. I don't even know if they'll let me stay with her in the hospital. If not, I'll just get a room nearby. There's no way I'm going to be hours away when she needs me.

I step into the lobby and motion to Evan. He jumps up and meets me at the exit doors. "What's happening?" he asks.

"They're moving her to Little Rock," I say, my long stride eating up the ground to where the truck is parked. "She needs more intense care than they can offer here. Something about ICU and pulmonology."

Evan nods. "What can I do?"

"Take me home. I need to pack."

The trip home passes in a blur. I can't help but wonder if the cancer is back. She's been doing so well—all her scans were clean—but there's always a chance of it returning.

"Do you need to call someone at your job?" Evan asks, pulling into the drive.

I get out my phone and pull up Bradley's number.

"Hello?"

"Hey, Bradley. I hate to do this, but my mom's in the hospital and they are moving her to Little Rock. Is there any way I can have the next week or two off?" I'm asking, because I really like my job, and hope that I'm able to come back to it, but Mom comes first.

"Of course," he says. "I don't know how much paid time off you've accrued, but don't worry about your job. We're almost done with the interior of the play center. We'll be fine without you for a couple of days. Take all the time you need."

Relief floods me. "Thanks. I . . . Thanks."

"You bet. Go take care of your mom. Let us know if there's anything you need."

I hang up and jump out of the truck. I rush up the sidewalk to my front door. Once I'm inside, I make sure things are set for me to be gone for a bit, and throw some clothes and necessities into a bag. I grab Mom's book and knitting supplies, just in case she starts feeling better and wants to have something to do.

"You want me to drive you down there?" Evan asks from his seat at the dining room table.

I startle at the sound of his voice. "I forgot you were still here."

He laughs. "Yeah, not surprised by that, actually. You've been half out of it since you called me."

I roll my head on my neck, trying to release some of the stress. "I'll be alright," I say. "I don't want to be a pain, and that's a long drive."

He stares at me for a minute before pushing to stand. "If you're sure."

I nod. "I'm sure. Thanks for everything today."

He walks over and pulls me into a hug, slapping his hand on my back. "I've got your back, brother. Let me know when you get there and keep me updated." He steps back.

"I will."

We step outside, and I lock up the house. I open the truck door and throw my bag into the passenger seat. Taking one last look at the house, I back out of the drive. It's going to be a long ten days.

CHAPTER FOURTEEN

Gabby

I pull into the driveway and put the Jeep in park. Glancing over at the flowers in the passenger seat, a fresh wave of tears starts to fall. How can he still love me? It's been so long since we broke up. I assumed he'd moved on, and had hoped that one day I would, too.

My phone buzzes with an incoming text. Seeing Heath's name, I turn the phone off. I'm not ready to talk to him just yet. Having him back in Piney Brook, asking for a second chance

. . . it's a lot.

I get out and grab the flowers. They'll need to be put in water. I bring them to my face and inhale their sweet scent, the riot of colors bringing a watery smile to my face.

After a hot shower, I pad to the kitchen in my oversized nightgown and fuzzy socks. I open the fridge and groan. Why is it so hard to remember to go grocery shopping? Grabbing a bowl and spoon from the cabinet, I opt for a bowl of cereal with the last of the milk.

I grab my phone to add milk to the running grocery list I keep in my notes. I press the button to power it up and tuck it into the pocket of my nightgown before grabbing my cereal and heading for the couch. A nice rerun of something light sounds great.

My phone chimes with unread messages. I see several from Heath and one from Karlee. Deciding it can wait until after I've eaten, I put the phone on the end table and pick up the remote, flipping to the streaming app and pulling up the Golden Girls.

An hour later, my eyes are drifting closed. I turn off the TV, take my bowl to the sink, and head to bed.

The next morning, I'm heading to work, so I grab my phone, but it's dead. I charge it on my way to the diner so I can check my messages when I'm on break later.

As I walk in the door, I'm met with somber faces. "What's going on?" I ask, looking between Ms. Daisy and Patty.

"Gabby," Ms. Daisy says. "Did you hear that Rosanna is in the hospital in Little Rock?" she asks.

My heart drops. "What?" I ask. "What do you mean she's in the hospital? Little Rock? Why so far away? What happened?"

Ms. Daisy gives me a watery smile. "You didn't know? She was transferred there last night. Bradley was just in here with his crew for breakfast. When Heath wasn't with them, I asked about him. Bradley told me what was going on."

I groan internally. She must have taken a turn after I saw Heath at the beach. I bet that's what all those texts were about last night. "Thanks for letting me know. Is it okay if I take a few minutes and give Heath a call?"

Ms. Daisy smiles and pats my arm. "Of course, dear." She turns to Patty. "Are you okay covering, or do you need me to take some tables?"

"I'm good," Patty says, shooting me a worried glance.

"I'll be back out as soon as I can."

"Here," Ms. Daisy says, handing me her keys. "Use the office. You'll have more privacy."

I push through the swinging doors to the back room, then open the office and drop into the black leather chair at the desk. Taking a deep breath, I get out my phone and pull up Heath's number. My finger hovers over the button. I should call, right? That's what a friend would do. But what if he doesn't want to hear from me?

Nerves make my hands shake. Deciding to take the easy way out, I close
his number and pull up our text thread.

Gabby: I just heard about your mom. Is she okay?

Now I wait. I start biting my nails, a habit I thought I'd finally broken.
Guess not. When my phone dings in my lap, I jump, almost stabbing myself
in the face with my jagged nail.

Heath: She's in the ICU. They expect her to make a full recovery, but
she's in bad shape right now.

I place my hand over my stomach. *She's in the ICU?* I drop my head back
onto the office chair. I have to go see her. I look over to the bulletin board
where Ms. Daisy posts the schedules. I'm supposed to work the next three
days. Maybe I can get one of the dinner shift servers to cover for me.

Gabby: Tell her we are all thinking of her. I'm going to come see her as
soon as I can.

I'm scanning the schedule to see who might be available to cover for me
when a knock on the door startles me out of my thoughts.

"Coming," I call out, standing and opening the door.

"Well?" Ms. Daisy asks.

"Heath says she's expected to recover, but she's in the ICU." I fold my
arms across my middle. Rosie's been like a mother to me all these years. I'm
so mad at myself for not checking those messages sooner.

She shakes her head. "Poor Rosie. She's been through so much the last
few years."

I nod. "Do you think Tamra might cover for me today and tomorrow?
I'd like to go see her."

Ms. Daisy steps to the desk and picks up the phone. "Let's call and ask."

My phone dings with an incoming text.

Heath: You don't need to do that. She'll be okay. I'm sure you're busy.

That stings. Of course I need to go see her. *Is he being short because of
yesterday, or is he just stressed?* I pause and take a breath. He's stressed.
How could he not be? His mom's in the ICU.

"Tamra says she can be here in an hour. Why don't you go ahead and go. I'll help Patty." Ms. Daisy pulls me in and hugs me tight. "She's going to be okay, but I know you'll feel better if you see for yourself."

Three and a half hours later, I'm parked in the hospital parking lot staring at the double doors. Three hours in the car is a long time to think. If I've learned anything these past few months going to cancer treatments and appointments with Momma A, it's that life is short and time is not guaranteed.

I take my time getting out of the car and walking inside the hospital. I've hated hospitals since Gram died seven years ago. Of course, part of that is because my mom had shown up playing the role of mourning daughter. Until she'd found out Gram didn't leave her anything in the will. I roll my eyes, remembering how she'd huffed and stormed out of Mr. Willis's office. Good riddance.

Stepping up to the reception desk, I wait my turn in line.

"Hi, I'm here to see Rosanna Atkins," I say when it's finally my turn.

"ID, please." The young woman behind the desk stretches out her hand. She takes my ID, makes a copy, and hands it back to me with a visitor's pass. "Room 411, down that hallway to the second set of elevators."

I nod, stick the badge to my shirt, and set off to find Momma A.

The fourth floor is quiet except for the occasional beeping from a monitor. I make my way down the corridor to room 411 and stop outside the doors. I'm nervous to see Heath again after the way we left things. I summon all my courage, and open the door.

Heath's head is resting on the edge of the hospital bed, a soft snore coming from him. "Hi," I whisper to Rosie when I catch her eye. She's got the oxygen mask on, so she just gives me a small wave. I walk to her side and take her hand in mine. "How are you feeling?"

"Gabby?" Heath says, lifting his head. "You came?"

I nod, not breaking eye contact with Rosie. "I did. I had to check on my bestie." I give her a small grin and chuckle when she rolls her eyes.

"You didn't have to do that," Heath says, standing and wiping his hands over his face.

"I know," I respond. "Why don't you go get something to eat and a cup of coffee? I'll sit with her for a while."

Heath shoves his hands in his pockets. "I'm okay, thanks."

"Go on. I promise I'll call you if anything happens." I hold my breath, watching his facial expressions as he wars with himself.

"I'll be back in a few minutes, okay?" He leans in and kisses Rosie on the cheek. "Ten minutes, tops."

Once he steps outside, I sit in the chair he was just resting in. I lean forward and take Rosie's hand in mine. "Now that he's gone, how are you really doing?" I ask.

She shrugs. "I'm okay," she says, her voice distorted slightly from the mask covering her face.

I squeeze her hand. "You've got the whole town worried about you. Ms. Daisy sends her best."

Rosie nods. "Thank you," she says before closing her eyes.

"I'll just sit here while you rest," I say, letting go of her hand and leaning back in the chair.

Ten minutes later, Heath comes walking through the thick wooden door with two cups of steaming hot coffee. "It's not the Coffee Loft, but it's not the sludge I've been getting from the vending machine down the hall either." He hands me a cup.

"She's been sleeping since just after you left," I whisper, setting the coffee on the small table beside her bed. "How are you holding up?"

He makes eye contact with me and raises one corner of his mouth. "I'm okay," he says. "Thanks for driving all the way down here."

I step forward and put my arms out. "Need a hug?"

He steps forward and wraps me in his warm arms, careful not to spill his coffee. "I'm sorry I pushed you yesterday," he whispers. "I'll take whatever you're willing to give. If that's friendship, then I'm a lucky man."

The smell of apple pie baking in the oven makes me smile. I love this time of year. Food, friends, festivities. My three favorite f's. Of course, I'd feel better if Heath and Momma A were back home. I've been checking in every few days since I left the hospital. I still haven't gotten up the nerve to call. I'm afraid I'll hear his voice and say too much, but now's not the time. I can't tell him I've spent the last week wondering what would have happened if, that day on the beach, I had admitted I still love him too. I'm not brave enough to say that maybe we could give it another try. I'm not convinced I'd survive it if he broke my heart again.

The timer buzzes, pulling me out of my thoughts. I slip on the shark-shaped mitt and grab the pie from the oven. After I set the pie on the cooling rack, I power up my phone to check in again.

Gabby: How is everything? Are you okay?

I set the phone on the counter and clean up the dishes while I wait for him to respond.

Heath: Mom's doing better. They said everything looked good overnight, so she can be released this afternoon.

Gabby: That's wonderful! Can I bring you two some dinner? I could swing by the diner and get your mom's favorite fried chicken.

Heath: Evan and Karlee have already offered. Thanks.

Disappointment hits me hard and fast.

Gabby: That's nice of them. Will you let me know when you two are settled in at home and she's up for visitors?

When he doesn't respond right away, I put my phone in my purse and head to the bedroom to get dressed. Lacey's brother Bryce is in town and Mrs. Chambers is having an early Thanksgiving celebration since he'll be playing with the NHL on Thanksgiving Day.

An hour later, I'm sitting in Lacey's dining room, sipping sweet tea, and waiting for her mom to join us at the table so we can eat. Bryce, who plays for the Denver Edge, is across the table from me. Growing up, hockey is all he could ever talk about. I eye him over the rim of my glass. I can't deny he's grown into a handsome man. He catches me looking and winks. I roll my eyes. As hot as he is, he doesn't hold a candle to Heath.

"So, Gabby, are you ready to give me a shot?" Bryce asks, joking. Or I hope he is. Dating my best friend's brother would just be weird.

Lacey scoffs. "Like she'd date a hockey player."

My brows furrow. "Why wouldn't I?" I ask, truly puzzled. If I liked someone, I'd hope their profession wouldn't be a deal breaker. That wouldn't be fair. Especially since I'm still waiting tables, and a lot of people look down on me for that.

"You wouldn't want to leave Piney Brook." Lacey shrugs like it's an obvious answer.

"I might," I say softly. Staying here, being so close to Heath . . . it's been hard.

Lacey chokes on her drink, coughing and sputtering. I reach over and slap her back. "You okay?"

Once she gets a hold of herself, she pins me with a stare. "You'd leave Piney Brook? Since when?"

I take another sip of my drink to buy me some time. "Things change," I say, not meeting her eyes. Thank goodness Mrs. Chambers breaks the awkwardness when she calls out that dinner is done.

Lacey, Bryce and I all get up, heading for the kitchen to help bring the dishes to the table. Once everything is in place on the table, we say grace, and Bryce makes short work of slicing the meat. Plates are made, and everyone settles into a comfortable silence as we eat.

"Let's all take turns sharing what we are thankful for this year," Mrs. Chambers suggests. "I'll go first. I'm thankful that both my children, and my bonus daughter, have joined me for dinner today."

I shift in my seat. Ever since Lacey and I became friends, her mom has gone out of her way to make me feel welcome. I think she felt sorry for me when she found out my mom didn't want me. It's appreciated, but it also reminds me of what I'm missing out on with my own mother.

"I'll go next," Bryce says, wiping his mouth and placing his napkin beside his plate. "I'm thankful that the Edge picked me up and offered me a contract."

I'm not surprised that hockey is what he's thankful for. He's getting his childhood wish.

"I guess it's my turn. I'm grateful for new opportunities and great friends," Lacey says.

All eyes turn to me. *What am I thankful for this year?* "I'm thankful for a good job, good friends, and that Mrs. Atkins is doing better."

"How is she?" Mrs. Chambers asks. "I've considered calling her, but I didn't want to be a bother."

"She's doing well. Heath said she's being released today." I take a bite of food, hoping that the warmth I feel in my cheeks doesn't show on my face.

"Has he figured out how much you like him yet?" Bryce asks. "It's a shame, if you ask me."

I swallow my food carefully to keep from spitting it on the plate. "I don't know what you're talking about," I lie.

"I wanted to ask you out your senior year, but I saw how you looked at him." Bryce shrugged. "Figured there wasn't any sense competing since you were already half in love with him."

"Bryce!" Lacey admonishes. "I told you never to ask out my friends. It's weird."

He gives her his signature smirk. The one that's all over sports tabloids. "Yeah, well. Hate to break it to you, little sister—you're not the boss of me."

"Well," Mrs. Chambers says, sliding her plate away from herself. "This has been enlightening. Why don't we move to the dessert Gabby brought us before her face catches fire?" She stands and takes her plate to the kitchen.

"All I'm saying is," Bryce continues, not taking the hint, "if you looked at me the way you look when you mention his name, I'd jump on that and never let you go."

My mouth drops open and closes again several times. I'm certain I look like a fish out of water, but I have no idea how to respond to that.

"He had his chance, and he blew it." Lacey stands, taking my plate and hers. "Too bad for him." She pins Bryce with a glare. "Do not ask my friends out." She shudders and walks to the kitchen with our dirty dishes.

"What did she mean by that?" Bryce asks.

"I'm pretty sure she meant I'm off limits," I say, debating putting my glass directly against my heated cheeks.

"No, the other part."

"I have no idea," I say. "Maybe she just means we aren't as close as we were before he left for the Army."

Bryce looks like he's about to ask something else when his mom calls him from the kitchen. "I'm not waiting for your dirty plate all day. Get in here and help bring out the dessert."

I'm not sure what Mrs. Chambers says to Lacey and Bryce in the kitchen, but thankfully the rest of the evening's conversation is much lighter and less embarrassing. My phone dings with an incoming message, just as I'm sliding my shoes on to leave.

"Wonder who that is," Lacey says, smiling.

"Probably Ms. Daisy," I say, sliding my coat on. "I'll check when I get home."

"Mm-hmm." She leans in and gives me a hug. "He was serious, you know. Bryce had the biggest crush on you when we were kids."

I pull back, surprised. "No way."

She nods. "I don't even think the fact that I threatened him would have stopped him from pursuing you. We saw you and Heath up at the lake one day senior year, and he knew he didn't stand a chance."

I shake my head. "We weren't together."

She smiles sadly. "You've always been his, even when you're too stubborn to let yourself believe it." She opens the door and I step outside.

"I don't think so," I hedge. My phone dings again with another incoming message.

"If you still feel anything for him, you both deserve a chance to figure out if you belong together." She gives me a small wave and closes the door.

The fact is, I still love Heath just as much today as I did back then, but a lot has changed. *Should I risk my heart again?* I don't know if I can.

CHAPTER FIFTEEN

Heath

"Make sure she takes it easy," the nurse says as she helps Mom into my truck. "She'll still feel weak for a while until she recovers."

I nod. "Absolutely."

The nurse makes sure Mom is settled comfortably and then closes the truck door.

"Thanks, Heath," Mom says, putting her seatbelt on. "I'm so ready to be in my own home."

I wait for her to be buckled before putting the truck in drive. "I know, Ma. Me too," I say.

Mom dozes most of the way back to our house. The drive is slower than it should be since everyone and their brother seems to be out on the roads today. I glance at the clock, hoping we make it before Evan and Karlee are due to deliver dinner. By the looks of it, we'll be lucky to be pulling into the driveway when they show up.

My back is screaming from sleeping in the pull-out chair in Mom's room the past few days. I didn't care how lumpy it was. I refused to leave her. Thankfully, my job at Lost Creek Construction is still safe. I've come to really enjoy working on Bradley's crew. He's been calling me every few days to check in and see if we needed anything. They even sent flowers to Mom's room.

We pull into the driveway a half hour later than I expected and see Evan's truck there already.

"Who's that?" Mom asks, waking up when I turn off the truck.

"Evan and Karlee brought us dinner." I step out of the truck and walk around the back to her side. The front door of the house swings open just as I'm helping Mom down.

"Here," Evan calls as he walks over to us. "Let me help." He lifts Mom up and carries her inside.

"Put me down, silly boy," Mom says, but there's a lightness in her tone that's been missing for too long. "You'll break your back."

"I'll do no such thing," Evan says, laughing. "I'm a big strapping man now, Momma A."

I follow them inside and watch as Evan lowers her into her chair. "See," he says, flexing his biceps. "Piece of cake."

Karlee laughs. "You better carry me across the threshold one day," she says, grinning. "Since you're so strong and everything."

He pulls her into a hug and dips her for a kiss. "I'll carry you anywhere you want to go."

Mom's eyes fill with tears and I wish I had a camera to capture the smile on her face. Unfortunately, my phone's still in the truck.

"I'll heat up dinner while you help Heath get everything out of the truck." Lacey kisses Evan's cheek and turns toward the kitchen. "Don't you worry about a thing, Mrs. Atkins," she says on her way out. "We've got it covered."

"You know," I say to Evan once we are outside. "I could have gotten this by myself."

He shakes his head. "Not according to my girl." He laughs. "Really, I think she wanted me to grill you about Gabby. Apparently, Lacey let it slip that she thinks Gabby is still in love with you."

The heavy feeling I've had in my chest since Gabby told me she didn't think we had a chance is back in full force at his words. "Nope," I say, popping the p. "The day Mom got sick, I ran into her at the lake, and she made it pretty clear she's not interested in being more than friends."

Evan shakes his head. "You sure about that?"

I shut the truck door and lean against it. "I wish it was different. I'd give anything to be with her again."

Evan stares at me a moment before his face breaks out into a huge grin. "So you *were* together before you left for the Army! I knew it!"

I rub my free hand over my face and groan. "Yeah, we were. We just didn't tell anyone. It doesn't matter anyway. I messed up. Now she doesn't want anything to do with me."

"We all mess up," Evan says. "If she's the one, show her."

"It's not that simple," I say. "She thought I was Zade's father."

"What? Why did she think that?" Evan asks.

"Because that's what someone told her, right after I broke up with her. It's a long, dumb story." I give him the short answer. If I could go back in time and change it, I would. "I won't keep pushing for something if she's not interested. I'm not that guy."

"You broke up with her? That was dumb."

"I know. I *said* it was dumb. I didn't want her waiting around for me. I thought I was being, well, nice."

Evan pats me on the shoulder. "So, be her friend for now. Show her that you're here. That you're not going anywhere. Maybe she'll change her mind."

"Maybe," I say. "I was actually thinking of moving back to Kentucky after the first of the year if I can convince Mom to come."

"You'd leave Piney Brook again?" Evan asks.

"I don't think I could stay here and watch her fall for someone else," I answer honestly.

"Guys, what's taking so long? Rosie and I are ready to eat," Karlee calls from the front door.

"Coming," Evan and I say at the same time.

We decide to eat in the living room, letting Mom rest in her chair. "Thank you for doing this," I say to Karlee.

"Hey, I helped," Evan says, tossing a roll at my head.

"Boys, no food fights. Remember the last time," Mom says, smiling. "I was cleaning mashed potatoes out of the dining room chairs for weeks. Every time I thought I got it all, I found another spot." She shakes her head and laughs. "You two were always up to something. It's so good to see you back together."

"For now, anyway," Evan says, shooting me a look.

"What was that dear?" Mom asks.

"Nothing," I say, cutting him off. "Evan's just worried that now that he has a girlfriend, I'll find a new best friend."

Karlee laughs. "Trust me, there's enough of him to go around." She kisses his cheek. "Besides, I'm not one of those girls that thinks my boyfriend shouldn't have a life outside of me."

"One in a million," I joke. "You sure you wouldn't rather marry me? I'm a veteran, after all."

Evan growls. "Stay away from my girlfriend."

"Chill out," I say, laughing. "I was joking."

"Heath wouldn't dare," Mom says, taking a bite of her chicken alfredo. "He loves Gabby too much."

I choke on my tea. "Mom!"

"What?" she asks innocently. "It's not like it's a secret."

Evan laughs. "She's got you there, man. Anyone with eyes can see you're in love with her."

Karlee claps her hands together. "I can't wait to tell Lacey!"

"No one is telling Lacey anything!" I nearly shout. "Gabby made it clear she's not interested."

Karlee giggles. "That's not what I heard when I was getting coffee the other day."

My head snaps in her direction. "What?"

She makes a motion like she's zipping her lips.

"Seriously, Karlee. This is important. Did she say she was interested in being with me?"

Karlee's eyes go wide, and she mumbles through closed lips.

"Fine, I get it. Girl code or something." I frown and push my plate away.

"Like I said," says Evan, taking Karlee's hand. "If she's the one, show her."

After they leave, I make sure Mom is settled for a while before I head to my room to unpack from the trip. I dump the bag onto my bed, and my phone bounces from the bed and lands at my feet. Evan's words echo in my head. "Show her."

I pick up the phone and send a text.

Heath: I hope you had a nice day. Mom and I are back home and settled in. I'm sure she'd love to see you any time.

I hit send and drop the phone onto my bed. Grabbing the dirty clothes, I head out to throw them into the washing machine. When I get back to my room, I check to see if she's messaged me back. I'm disappointed when I don't see a message from her. "Show her," runs through my mind again.

Heath: I would love to see you.

There, that's showing her, right?

Things used to be so easy between us. We'd been friends forever before we kissed the first time. The memory washes over me as if it were yesterday. Gabby in her lavender prom dress with butterflies adorning the tulle skirt and top. She looked like a fairy wrapped in cotton candy. It stole my breath away. We went to prom as friends. Neither one of us even considered going with someone else. The DJ played Ed Sheeran's "Perfect," and I realized how much I cared for her. It changed everything.

Holding her in my arms, swaying in time with the music, I realized I never wanted to let her go. She held my heart in the palm of her hand. So, when I dropped her off at home, I couldn't help but lean in and kiss her. The moment our lips met, it was like coming home. I never wanted to stop, but her grandma flipped on the porch light and we'd jumped apart like we'd been caught doing something wrong. Except kissing her felt like the only right thing I'd done all my life.

After that, things started to change, and by the end of the summer, we were together. When she asked if we could keep it between us, I should have said no. I wanted to yell from the rooftop and let everyone know she was mine.

I knew her mother had hurt her deeply, and I vowed to myself I'd never hurt her like that. In the end, I hurt her anyway.

I bring my fingers to my lips, remembering the way hers felt pressed against mine. If there is a chance she feels the way I do, I have to see this through. She's been hurt too much. I can't blame her for trying to protect herself. If it takes time to prove to her that I'm here to stay, I will be the most patient man in history.

My phone dings with an incoming message, and I rush to grab it.

Gabby: I could come Sunday after work and bring dinner. For three?

Well, it's not a profession of love, but it's something.

Heath: Sounds perfect. I can't wait.

The next few days are going to feel like an eternity.

CHAPTER SIXTEEN

Gabby

My heart races and my hands shake when I pull into the driveway at Rosie's. I'm second-guessing myself. After the dinner with Lacey's family, I'd decided to open my heart to the possibility of something more with Heath, but now . . . I'm not so sure. I put the car in park and rest my head on the steering wheel. When I look back up, Heath is standing in the doorway.

Seeing him takes my breath away and pushes my reservations to the back of my mind. In this moment, I realize Lacey is right. If there's something there, we should explore it. I take a deep breath to steady my nerves and open the door.

"Hey," I say, as Heath walks up to the Jeep.

"Hey," he says, reaching his hands out to take the bag of food. "Anything else?"

I shake my head. "No, just the one bag." I put my purse over my shoulder and step down from the Jeep.

Heath reaches around me and shuts the door. "Thank you for coming. I've been looking forward to this for days." He smiles. "So has Mom."

I nod. My stomach is doing somersaults. "Me too," I admit.

That makes his smile light up his whole face. I've missed that look—Heath genuinely happy.

"Let's get this inside," he says, holding up the bag.

"Right," I say. Stepping into the house and sliding off my flats, I call, "Momma A?"

"In here," she calls back from the living room.

Heath steps in beside me and motions for me to go ahead of him. In the living room, Rosie's in her favorite chair, a crocheted blanket on her legs. She looks tired, but healthy.

"Gabby brought dinner. Do you want to eat in here?" Heath asks.

"Please, if you two don't mind," she says. "Heath, why don't you go get everything together while Gabby and I catch up?"

Heath pauses, looking back and forth between us. "Uhh . . . Will you two be okay?"

"Go ahead," I say. "We'll be fine."

He nods and heads off toward the kitchen.

"Now," Rosie says. "I need to know. Do you still love my son?"

My mouth goes dry and my palms start to sweat. "Well, I, uhm . . ." I sigh and sink back into the couch. "I do, but it's not that simple."

She shakes her head. "You kids always complicate things. Of course it's that simple."

"He hurt me," I say.

She nods. "He did. You hurt him, too. When you cut ties."

Wait, what? "*He* broke up with *me*," I argue.

"Yes, but you cut him out of your life. You two had been best friends for a lot longer than you'd been an item. You both lost a friend that day."

I'm not sure why I feel like the tables have turned, but my goodness, I didn't expect this tonight. "That's true. But I heard about Olivia that day, too, and felt like I'd been replaced. Honestly, though, if I had known the truth back then, I'm not sure if I would have chosen differently. I've grown a lot since then, but I obviously still have trust issues."

She looks at me for a moment. "You both were hurt back then. But if you can forgive each other now—and forgive yourselves—for the past, you might find happiness *now*. Can you forgive and let the future play out how it will?"

Can I truly forgive and look to the future instead of holding onto the hurts of the past? "I think so, yes."

"It's time to let go of the past," she says softly.

Before I can answer, Heath steps back into the living room. He looks from me to his mom and groans. "Mom, what did you say to Gabby? Why does she look like she's ready to bolt?"

"I'm sure I don't know what you're talking about," she says, looking at Gabby. "We were just talking about the future."

I paste on a smile and nod my head in agreement. "She's right. I'm ready for dinner," I say, taking the plate Heath is holding out for me. "It smells delicious."

After we eat, Rosie says she is ready to go lie down.

"Will you stay while I help her to her room?" Heath asks.

I nod. "I'd love to."

While he's gone, I think about what Rosie said. We both hurt each other. Back then, all I could see was how he'd hurt me. Now, I can see clearly that by blocking him out of my life, I was as guilty as he was. Something about that makes opening my heart a little less terrifying.

"Thanks for waiting," Heath says, coming back into the room and sitting beside me on the couch.

"No problem," I say, smiling. "I actually wanted to talk, if that's okay?"

Heath shifts on the couch so he's facing me more fully. "Of course."

"I think I owe you an apology," I say, looking at my hands in my lap. "All this time, I could only see how you hurt *me*. Your mom helped me realize that I hurt you, too. Part of me will always be that abandoned child, determined to protect herself from rejection, but I'm learning. I'm sorry I pushed you out of my life."

Heath shakes his head. "No, Gabby. That was all on me. Of course, I'd have loved it if you hadn't cut ties, but I should have made sure you were my priority and I failed. I'm so sorry."

A tear slips down my cheek, and I wipe it away. "Your mom said it's time to let go of the past, and I think I agree."

"So what does that mean?" Heath asks, his voice quiet.

I lean back on the couch and smile at him. "I think it means we work on getting to know each other again."

He smiles at me and reaches for my hand. "You know how I feel," he says, lacing his fingers through mine.

"I do." I squeeze his fingers gently with mine. "Want to watch a movie?"

He stares at me for a moment. "Princess Bride?" he asks.

"Of course," I say, grinning at him.

"As you wish." He grabs the remote from the coffee table and finds the movie on one of the streaming services. He scoots closer to me and presses play. We hold hands the entire movie, and I'm transported back to when things were easy between us. When falling in love happened so gradually that we didn't even notice at first.

"Okay," Lacey says, plopping a bag on the counter. "I've got all the things we need for our mocktails."

I grin at her, pulling the fancy glasses down from the cabinet. "Perfect," I say, setting them on the counter. "Anne should be here anytime. She's bringing pizza."

Lacey nods. "Karlee texted she's on her way with cucumber slices and face masks."

I do a little dance in the kitchen. "It's been too long since we've had a mocktail party," I say, adding ice to the glasses.

"You're not wrong," she says.

A few minutes later, Anne and Karlee come through the door together. "Time to party!" Anne shouts, raising the pizza boxes above her head and doing a little shimmy.

Everyone laughs and I take the pizza boxes and put them onto the counter beside the plates I'd taken out earlier.

"Who's ready for a drink?" Lacey asks, motioning to the counter where her supplies are all laid out.

"Me!" Karlee says. "What are our options?"

"We've got the stuff to make Pina Colada, Citrus Fizz, Sweet Sunrise, and a Cinderella."

"Oh, those sound good," Anne says. "I vote for the Cinderella. I could get down with being a girl who finally finds her prince."

I shake my head. "These two," I say, waving my hand between Karlee and Lacey, "already have their Prince Charmings."

"Hey," Karlee says. "You could have yours too, anytime you wanted. I know Heath is all in. You should have seen him when we took them dinner the night Mrs. A came home from the hospital and she let it drop that he's still in love with you."

Lacey smacks my arm affectionately. "See, I *told* you!"

"So it's just lil' ole me without a Prince Charming, now?" Anne says dramatically. "I see how it is."

"Can we please make a drink and have some pizza before we gang up on me about my love life?" I ask, pouting.

"Four Cinderellas coming right up!" Lacey makes quick work of the drinks, and we pile our plates with pizza before heading to the living room where I've turned on the top-hits music station.

"So, we have drinks, and pizza," Karlee says. "Spill it!"

I shake my head. "And you say you're my friends," I say, grinning.

"Uh-huh. You're stalling," Anne says. "What's the status?"

"Heath and I are friends. We are getting to know each other as the adults we are."

"So, does that mean you're spending time together? Dating?" Lacey asks.

I shrug. "I'm not sure what to call it," I say honestly. "We watched a movie after his mom went to bed a few days ago."

Lacey's eyes go wide. "What movie did you watch?"

I blush. "Princess Bride."

She claps her hands. "They're getting together!"

"I wouldn't go there," I say.

"Did you cuddle?" Karlee asks.

Why are my friends so perceptive? "Not really," I hedge.

"What does that mean?" Anne asks. "That's pretty much a yes or no question, don't you think?"

Lacey and Karlee nod in agreement.

"We held hands," I say before taking a huge bite of pizza.

The girls high five each other.

"What's that about?" I ask around the food in my mouth.

"We knew it was a matter of time. Now, anyone want to guess who gets engaged first?" Anne asks.

"What?" Karlee asks, surprise on her face. "Who said anything about getting engaged?"

"Oh, come on," Anne says. "You and Evan have marital bliss written all over you."

"It's only been four months," she says, frowning. "I was with Patrick for years."

Lacey grins. "Yeah, but he was the wrong one for you."

"What about you?" Karlee says, pointing at Lacey. "You could be engaged before all of us. Knox seems to be all in."

Lacey sputters. "We'll see, I guess. Are we doing facials or what?"

We all laugh. "Can we eat first?" Anne asks. "I'm actually starving."

After the pizza and our Cinderellas are gone, Lacey makes up a batch of Sweet Sunrise, and we all pick a face mask.

"This is just what I needed," I say, careful not to move my mouth and mess up the mask, or knock the cucumber slices off my eyes. "It's been a stressful few months."

"Agreed," Anne says. "Who knew taking over the salon would be so stressful. I've worked there most of my life."

"Being in charge is different than working there," I say, remembering how inadequate I felt trying to learn to place the weekly order at the diner.

"You're not wrong," she says, sighing.

Once we are sufficiently relaxed, we clean up and settle in to watch a movie. I'm so grateful for these women sitting in my living room. Since Gram died, I've felt alone. I miss her more this time of year. Christmas was always my favorite holiday, but Halloween was hers. She'd go all out decorating, buying full-sized candy bars for the older kids and snack-sized ones for the younger ones.

When the end credits are rolling, Lacey stands and stretches. "I think it's time for me to go."

Anne and Karlee stand and stretch, before moving to grab their things.

"Thanks for this," I say. "I needed a girls' night."

"Anytime," Lacey says. "Besides, we've all been wondering about you and Heath. It was a good way to get the scoop." She winks and puts her purse over her shoulder.

"If you guys find a good guy roaming around out there, send them my way," Anne says, as she steps out the front door.

"You got it," I call.

Closing the door behind them, I realize I have people in my corner. More than just Lacey. The thought startles me. I thought I was being careful not to let people in, and yet . . .

CHAPTER SEVENTEEN

Heath

When Gabby asked to watch a movie, and then let me hold her hand, the hope I'd been careful to keep contained took hold in my chest. There's still a chance for us, I know it.

Heath: Interested in grabbing dinner with me?

It's been a few days since the movie night, and it's been too long. I want to be with her always. Hold her hand and kiss her lips. It had taken everything in me to keep from giving her a goodnight kiss. We aren't there yet, but I hope we are soon. I'm staring at my phone, so I notice right away when the message goes from sent to read and the text bubble with the dots pops up.

Gabby: What are you thinking?

Yes! I've got a date!

Heath: How about I pick you up at six, and I'll surprise you?

That's a gamble. One thing I remember about Gabby is she does not like surprises.

Gabby: A surprise? [frowny face emoji]

I laugh. I knew she'd respond like that.

Heath: Please?

Gabby: Okay, but what should I wear?

A vision of Gabby in her prom dress pops into my head. Unrealistic, especially for what I have in mind.

Heath: Dress comfortably. Nothing too fancy.

I can hear the wheels turning in her head from here and it makes me smile.

Gabby: Okay, see you at six.

"You done texting your girl?" Hudson asks, tossing a paint roller at me. "We've got work to do."

I laugh and tuck my phone into my pocket. "Yeah, yeah. We have one wall to paint before we're finished with this project." The Coffee Loft is now connected to the play center with a glass door separating the two spaces. We're just finishing the paint and this job is done.

"Any idea why Bradley isn't here today?" I ask.

Hudson laughs. "Man, you missed a show!"

"I did?" I ask, confused.

"Apparently the owner of the Coffee Loft really doesn't like Bradley, and would only allow him to be on her side of the building for the door install."

I shake my head. "No way, Aurora is too sweet for that."

"I absolutely am not," she says, coming up behind me.

"Sorry," I say, blushing.

She laughs. "It's okay. Bradley and I go way back, and he was a bully when we were kids. I'd rather not deal with that."

"Really?" I ask. "That surprises me."

She puts one hand on her hip and pins me with a look that I'm sure would kill if looks really could. "Oh, really? Everyone said he was only mean to me, so I suppose you wouldn't understand."

"Why would he be mean to you?" I ask, truly confused. "I don't get it."

"I have no idea. You'd have to ask him," she says before walking away to help a customer.

Hudson busts out laughing. "That wasn't awkward at all!"

"Nope," I say. "Back to work."

At four o'clock, we wrap it up. The paint is finished, and as long as no one touches it until it's dry, that should be the end of this project.

"Any idea what's next?" I ask Hudson as we clean up our mess.

"I think Bradley said something about a vet's office going into the old bank building, but I'm not sure."

That would be good. For as long as I can remember, people have been driving their pets forty-five minutes into Lost Creek to the large animal vet there. Having one closer would be great.

"All right," I say, once we are all cleaned up. "I'm out of here."

"Big plans?" Hudson asks, a knowing grin on his face.

"Yep," I say, grinning from ear to ear.

"Good luck, man."

"Thanks," I say, surprised that he's not giving me a hard time. "See you tomorrow."

I pull into Gabby's driveway at 5:55. I didn't want to be late. I just hope she likes what I have planned.

I wait in the truck until just before six, then get out and walk up the steps to her front door and knock.

The door swings open, and I almost swallow my tongue. "You look beautiful," I say when I find my voice. Gabby's in a cream-colored sweater, a pair of jeans that fits her just right, and brown knee-high boots. The girl I left that summer has grown into a beautiful woman, and she's going out with me. Wow.

"Thanks," she says shyly. "Can I know where we are going yet?"

I shake my head and wait for her to lock her door. I walk her to the truck and open her door, helping her inside. "You'll see soon," I say, closing her door.

A few minutes later, we're driving down the road, and Gabby is guessing every two minutes. "Nope," I say again.

Finally, we get where we are going and I pull into the parking lot.

"Pizza and Playtime?" she asks. "Really?"

Oh no! I was hoping this would be fun. "We can go somewhere else if you'd rather." I shrug, trying not to let her see my disappointment. It's been forever since I've been to an arcade. It hadn't seemed fun without her by my side.

"Oh, no! If you're up for getting beat at Skee-Ball, that is." She grins and opens the truck door. "If you recall, I'm the best at that game."

Relief floods me. "Who says I haven't gotten better over the years?" I ask, meeting her at the front of the truck.

She raises an eyebrow and stares me down. "I'll take my chances," she says, smiling.

"Before we go in . . ." I say, hesitating. "Where do we land on holding hands?"

She smiles and a blush blooms on her cheeks. "I think that's okay."

"Are you sure? People will talk." I hold my breath, wishing on every star I've ever seen that she'll say it's okay.

"I know," she says, shrugging. "I don't want to hide. If that's okay? If we are dating . . . Are we not dating?" she asks.

"No, we're definitely dating," I say, taking the in she gave me.

"Okay, then, we're dating, and I don't want to hide that."

I link our fingers together and draw her hand to my mouth, placing a kiss on the back of it. "That sounds perfect."

I open the door and let her walk in ahead of me. At the counter, we place our order and get our game tokens. "Ready for me to beat you at Skee-Ball?" Gabby asks.

"Are you sure you want to start there?" I ask.

"Absolutely," she says, grabbing my hand and pulling me to the back corner where the game is set up.

It doesn't take long to see she's still more skilled at this game than I'll ever be. After she beats me three times in a row, I raise my hands in surrender. "Okay, okay. You are the undisputed winner!"

She cheers and hugs me. Holding her in my arms feels so right, I don't want to let go, but the buzzer for our food goes off in my pocket.

"Food's ready," she says, stepping back and pointing at my pocket.

"I'll get it, you want to find us a seat?"

She leans in and kisses my cheek. "Thanks for being a good sport," she says, then walks away to get a table.

I head to the counter to pick up our pizza and drink cups before joining her at a booth in the back of the dining area.

"I hope you're hungry," I say, setting the pie on the table. "I forgot how big these pizzas are."

"I'm starving. Seems winning makes me hungry," she teases.

"Uh-huh, rub it in," I say. "What would you like to drink?"

She opts for diet cola, and I head to the drink station to fill up our cups and grab some plates.

A few minutes later, we are on our second slice, laughing and talking like we used to. "I've missed this," I say, taking her hand in mine.

"Me too." She smiles and leans forward a bit.

I'm leaning in to kiss her, my heart racing and my palms sweating like they did that spring when we shared our first kiss. Gabby closes her eyes as she leans in toward me, and I sigh. I've dreamed of this kiss for years. I feel a lock of her hair brush against my cheek, and her hot breath mingling with mine. Our lips are almost touching . . .

"Well," Mrs. Govney says loudly. "I see you two are finally together. I must say, though, Heath, I expected you to retire from the Army, not quit."

"Hello, Mrs. G. It's nice to see you, too," I say. "I came home because it was time."

She shakes her head and gives me the same look she used to give me when I was caught in the hallway after the bell rang. "Mm-hmm."

"Well, this was lovely," Gabby says, sliding out of the booth. "I think we have another game to play. It was nice seeing you again, ma'am."

She pulls my hand, and I slide out after her. "I'll be sure to tell Mom you said hi."

With that, we walk away from the grumpiest woman I've ever known. And I've known some grumpy women.

"Good grief," Gabby says, moving to the air hockey table. "You'd think it was her mission to make everyone miserable or something."

I laugh. "She's good at it."

"Want to try your hand at air hockey, or are you tired of losing?"

I won the first round. Then lost the next two. "Okay, I think I'm done losing for the night," I say. "Ready for the next part of our date?"

"Next part?" Gabby asks.

"Yep, we have one more stop to make." I grin. "And before you even ask, no I'm not telling you."

Fifteen minutes later, we pull up in front of the abandoned Dollar General on the far side of town. It's been converted to a temporary "Spooky Halloween" store, as the banner strung above the entrance proclaims.

"What are we doing here?" Gabby asks.

"I figured you'd like to see if there's anything new to add to Gram's collection. My treat."

Her mouth drops open. "You remembered?"

I take her hand in mine and lean over to place a kiss on her cheek. "I remember everything," I remind her.

Gabby takes her time walking up and down each aisle in the store before finally settling on a pumpkin that blows up and has lights inside it. "I don't want anything too scary," she says.

"It's perfect," I say, taking the box from her. "Anything else?"

She shakes her head. "I've already got haystacks and the candy."

I'm not surprised. Gabby's always prepared for the holidays. "Should we pay then?"

She nods and takes my free hand as we walk to the register. I could get used to this.

CHAPTER EIGHTEEN

Gabby

I can't remember when I've had so much fun on a date . . . which could be because I don't date. Not really. I've tried once or twice over the years, but it never felt right. It was always awkward and forced. Tonight I felt free. I know word will be around town by morning that we were together and holding hands, but I don't really care. What I said was true—I don't want to hide us. Not this time.

We pull into my driveway, and Heath turns to me.

"Can I walk you to your door?"

I nod. "That would be great." He gets out of the truck and walks around to my side, opening the door for me and helping me down, then he grabs the box from the store with one hand.

I slide my fingers into his as we walk slowly toward the front porch. The light is on, and it reminds me of our first kiss. I chuckle.

"What's funny?" Heath asks.

"I was remembering our first kiss when Gram threw on the porch light and scared us both to death."

Heath laughs. "I remember. I felt like a kid who'd just stolen the best candy in the world."

I smile up at him. "That's sweet."

"Not as sweet as I remember your lips being that night. That was the best kiss I've ever had."

The surprise must show on my face because he chuckles. "I've only ever kissed one other person since you. Let's just say it wasn't what dreams were made of."

I nod. "I get it."

He stops when we reach the front door and sets the box down on a porch chair. "You do?"

"Yeah. Well, kind of. I've been on two dates, and both of them were so bad we never even got to the kissing part."

Heath lets out a relieved sigh. "I'm sorry. But I'm glad none of them worked out, or I wouldn't be able to be here with you now."

He pulls me in for a hug, and I lean into his warmth. A feeling of rightness washes over me. "I'm glad you didn't find someone else either. I'm not sure my heart would have been able to take it."

He holds me tighter before pulling back slightly. "Do you think . . . Can I kiss you?" he asks.

Am I ready for that? "Yes," I whisper.

Heath reaches up, gently moving a strand of hair away from my face. "I've dreamed about this kiss," he whispers, his eyes on mine.

I bring my hands up, cradling his face in my palms. "Kiss me?"

When our lips come together, it's everything I remember, and much more. The softness of his lips on mine feels heavenly. The way he kisses me, so gentle and sweet, takes my breath away. This kiss feels like a promise. Warmth consumes me, and I lean into him more. We are connected, his arms wrapped around me and his face in my hands, and it feels like we are where we are meant to be. In each other's arms.

"Wow," I say, bringing my fingers to my lips when we part. "That was perfect."

Heath smiles. "You're perfect," he says, stepping back. "When can I see you again?"

"How about this weekend? I'm off by two on Saturday. Feel like helping me get the Halloween boxes from the attic and decorating?"

"I'd love to."

He waits for me to unlock the door, and moves the box inside. Then turns and heads to his truck. "Get inside," he calls out the window. "So I know you're safe from the trash pandas that roam these streets."

I laugh and head inside, closing and locking the door behind me before leaning against it, a huge smile on my face.

Saturday can't come soon enough.

Heath's just handed me down the last box from the attic when his phone rings. "Hello," I hear him say. I move away from the attic stairs, trying not to eavesdrop on his conversation. His voice goes soft and sweet, like it did when he asked if he could kiss me on the front porch. After ten minutes of trying to distract myself by fiddling with the boxes, he's still talking in those soothing tones. I can't help myself—I step closer.

"I know. I love you too, Olivia," Heath says.

My heart drops. I move away from the stairs and set the box on top of the others. I can't do this. Not again. Those words, in that tone, to her. I knew they were close, and that he cared for her, but I won't compete with another woman.

I always lose.

Grabbing my keys and my purse, I head out the front door. I need time to think. I hop in the car and drive. Not caring where I'm going. How could we be right back where we started?

Tears start falling down my cheeks, and I pull off the highway onto a lookout area, and park the car. Getting out, I wander down the path that's marked for a nature trail, and let the tears fall.

By the time I reach the end of the trail and turn back, I've mulled it over and over in my brain. Could I have overreacted? I really don't know. Olivia and Zade's dad had seemed so happy at Heath's birthday party. They'd behaved like a couple in love.

Heath had said I was his priority, and that he'd only ever kissed one other person. I wonder if it was Olivia. Maybe I should have asked, but if I'm being honest, I didn't want to know.

Rosie's words come back to me. "It's time to let go of the past." How do I even do that? I sit on a bench and look out over the trail. Something Gram said about Pops floats through my mind. "The secret to a relationship like the one Pops and I had is communication. We learned to not make assumptions. We talked things out. Especially when it was hard."

I look to the sky. "Thanks, Gram."

I finish the trek back to the Jeep and pull my phone from the glove box where I'd stuffed it so I wasn't tempted to look at it.

I've got several missed calls and texts.

Heath: Where'd you go?

Heath: What happened? Gabby, you're worrying me.

Heath: I love you. I'll be here when you get back.

Heath: If I don't hear from you soon, I'm getting a search party together.

That last one was two minutes ago. I hit reply.

Gabby: I'm on my way home. We need to talk.

I drop my phone into my purse and turn the Jeep back towards home. Thirty minutes later, I'm parked in the driveway when Heath comes rushing out the front door.

"Where have you been? I've been worried sick!"

I nod. "I know, and I'm sorry. I freaked out."

He wraps his arms around me for a second, then pulls back. "You what? Why?" Heath looks so confused and hurt.

"Let's go inside."

He follows me into the house, shutting the door behind us. I sit on the couch and take a deep breath.

"I heard you on the phone with Olivia." I watch his face for anything that would help me understand where we are.

"Okay," he says. "I still don't understand."

He seems genuine, but I need to get the rest out. "I heard you tell her that you love her the same way you say it to me."

He shakes his head and plops down into the chair across from the couch. "So you heard me tell my friend that I love her, and assumed . . . "

"It was the *way* you said it," I argue.

"I was being soothing. She and Dominic had just gotten into an argument and he'd walked out."

"Oh," I say, dropping my head into my hands.

"I do love her. Like a friend or a sister. I've told you that. The love I have for you definitely doesn't fall into that same category."

I nod. "I'm so sorry. I assumed the worst."

"Yeah, you did. I want this with you, Gabby. I want to be all in. I want forever, a house, kids, everything."

My head whips up. "What?"

"Let me finish," he says. "I want it all, but you have to want it, too. Enough to trust me. You can't keep shutting me out and running away all the time."

"I . . . I don't know what to say. For so long, I've tried to protect myself by shutting people out before they can hurt me."

He nods. "I know that. I know you. But by now, you should know that there's no one else for me but you. No one."

Tears prick the backs of my eyes, and my nose starts to run. "I'm sorry," I say again. "The only thing I can say is that I'll try. When I was walking the trail, something Gram said to me about communication popped into my head. It's why I came back."

Heath nods his head.

I take a deep breath and push it out. "I want this with you too. I want to see where this goes, but I can't promise I'll never freak out, or shut down."

Heath stands up. "I want you to be confident in my love for you. I want *you*. All of you. But if you can't trust me, it's not going to last. And I want us to last."

The tears start to fall. "I want to trust you," I say. "I want to let go of the past. I'm just still learning how."

Heath sits beside me on the couch and takes my hand. "I'd change your past if I could, but I can't. I'm willing to put in whatever time and patience you need me to, but I want to know you're willing to do what it takes, too. You have to decide if you trust me. If you can stick around when times get tough. Because, I'm telling you now, things will get tough at some point. That's life. I need a partner who will be by my side."

He leans in and kisses my cheek. "I'm going to go. I need some space to think, and you do, too. Call me when you're ready."

He stands and walks out the door, taking my bruised heart with him.

CHAPTER NINETEEN

Heath

It's been two days since I left Gabby's house, and with every hour that passes, my heart sinks. I'd hoped we were on the same page. Then, at the first sign of trouble, she left. Shut me out. I went from worried, to scared, to hurt and back to scared before she'd texted me back.

Olivia had called me crying. Apparently, she and Dominic had gotten into an argument and he'd stormed out. I was trying to console her, but in the process, I'd hurt Gabby's feelings. Again. I had no clue that she would assume I was in love with Olivia. I thought we'd cleared that up.

What really stung was that she walked out instead of talking to me about it. I love her with all my heart, but I can't see a future with her if she leaves every time things get hard. I don't want a marriage like my parents had. I don't want to wonder if one day she'll leave and never come back. I wouldn't survive it.

My phone rings, and my heart jumps into my chest. *Please be Gabby.*

Olivia. I swipe to answer and put the phone on speaker, laying it on the bed next to me. "Hello?"

"Heath, I'm glad I caught you."

"What up?" I ask, not really in the mood to talk to anyone. "Is Zade okay?"

Olivia pauses. "He's fine. What's wrong?"

"Nothing," I lie. "Is everything okay?"

"Yeah, I was just calling to let you know that Dominic and I talked it out. He just needed some time to blow off steam so he didn't overreact and hurt my feelings. He said he needed time to think it through."

"He should have stayed there and talked it out," I say, firmly.

"Haven't you ever needed space to think before you talk about something that hurt you?" she asks.

Have I? "I don't think running away solves anything."

"Uh-huh. Care to tell me what's going on?" she asks.

I groan. "Gabby overheard me telling you I loved you and freaked out. She left without a word. I was worried. When she came back and explained what happened, I felt sick. You know about my dad. How can I sign on for a relationship with someone who may up and leave one day with no warning? I can't."

Olivia is quiet for too long. "Olivia?"

"I'm here. I'm just thinking about how to respond to that."

Great. That means she thinks I'm wrong. "Go ahead. Don't sugarcoat it."

"I can see where you're coming from, but try to put yourself in her shoes. She heard you tell another woman you loved her. Without context."

"She should know by now that I love you and Zade. You're family to me," I argue.

"Right, but given our history, I could see why that would make her feel insecure." Olivia sighs. "Maybe she needed time to think before she talked to you. Maybe, deep down, she knew she was taking it out of context and needed some time to come to grips with what she knew and how she felt."

I consider what she's saying.

"You're ignoring something pretty important here," she says.

"I am?"

"She came back. She wanted to talk it through and hear your side."

When I don't respond, she continues. "If she was going to shut you out, she would have asked you to be gone when she got back."

"I hadn't considered that. All I could think was that she was holding on to the past and would never fully trust me again. I got scared."

"Mm-hmm, and she was probably scared that her worst nightmare was coming true. That you had feelings for me this whole time and she'd been right to shut you out the first time."

I groan. "So what now?"

"Well, that depends on how you left it," she says.

"I told her to call me when we've both cooled down."

"So, you left her. When she opened up and bared her soul to you?"

Shoot. "When you say it like that, it sounds really bad." Did I make her feel like I was abandoning her?

Olivia laughs. "Yeah, well. It sounds like you both could have handled that situation better."

"You're right." I sigh. "So, things with Dominic are really okay?"

"Yes. We talked everything out and we both feel a lot better. I think we both agree that it would be good for our family if I leave the Army when my contract is up."

Olivia and I spend the next few minutes discussing how it feels to leave the Army. It's not as easy as people might think. You miss the structure. But she and Dominic want to expand their family, and with Zade's health issues, Dominic really wanted her to leave. After they talked it out, they both agreed it was what was best for their family. She'd just needed time to wrap her head around it.

"Heath," Olivia says at the end of our conversation. "You need to cut yourself *and* Gabby some slack. You're going to have to learn how each of you needs to communicate. You both need to learn to give each other space to process. Fix this with her. She's good for you."

"Thanks for the advice," I say. "Talk to you soon."

I hang up the phone and throw my arm over my face. Will things always be this hard?

The next day, after work, I stop into Piney Brook Flowers and get a bouquet of lilies. Olivia's right. If Gabby was shutting me out, she wouldn't have asked to talk. She'd needed time to think. It doesn't change the fact that I need her to communicate that, but it does mean that maybe I overreacted too.

I place the flowers in the passenger seat, and head to her house. If she's not there, I'll leave the flowers and a note. When I called the diner earlier, I asked

Ms. Daisy what time she got off work. She should be home by now, unless she went somewhere else.

I pull into her driveway and park behind her Jeep. Thank goodness.

Grabbing the flowers, I step out of the truck and make my way to the front porch. Before I can knock, the door swings open and Gabby's sad eyes greet me.

"Heath." Her lip trembles like she's trying not to cry. "What are you doing here?"

"I think we've had enough time to think, don't you?" I ask, holding out the flowers.

Gabby shakes her head. "I can't do this. I can't go back and forth. It hurts too much."

I pull her into my arms. "I know. It hurts me, too. Can we please talk?"

She steps out of my arms and into the house. "Sure."

"Do you have a vase I can put these in?" I ask, holding up the bouquet.

"In the kitchen," she says, walking that direction. She pulls a vase down from the cabinet and fills it with water. "They smell so good," she says, taking them from me and bringing them to her face. She smiles as she places them inside the glass vase. "They're beautiful. Thank you."

"Not as beautiful as you."

She shakes her head again and draws her arms across her chest. She looks down, then at the ceiling, and sighs. She finally looks at me for a moment. "Love shouldn't hurt like this," she whispers.

I take her hand, pleased when she lets me guide her to the couch. "I talked to Olivia yesterday."

She looks up at me, her eyes glistening with tears.

"She said some things that made me realize I was wrong to be upset with you."

A lone tear slides down her cheek. I reach out and swipe it away with my thumb. "She said if you were really shutting me out, you wouldn't have asked to talk."

Gabby nods. "I didn't mean to shut you out, I needed to think."

"I understand that now. It just scared me. All I could think about was all the times my dad left after he and Mom argued. He came back at first, too. Until one day, he didn't." I take a deep breath. "But you're not him, and I can't hold what he did against you."

More tears fall, and I want to wipe each one away, but I keep my hands in my lap. I need to give her space to process. When did Olivia become a relationship expert?

"And I can't hold what my mom did against you." Gabby sighs. "I've been protecting myself by running away for so long it's a habit. I can't promise you that I won't need space to think sometimes. I'm sorry."

I reach out and take her hands in mine. "I know. It would help me if you would tell me when you need time alone. Are you okay with working on that?"

She takes her time answering, and I wait for her to be ready.

"I think I can do that."

I give her hands a squeeze. "And I'll give you the space you need. I promise."

She leans her head against my shoulder. "Are we okay?"

I wrap my arm around her and pull her close. "I want to be. What do you want?"

She's quiet for a while, and I start to worry, my mind running circles.

"I want that too," she says softly.

We sit like that for a while, just soaking each other in, before her stomach growls. "Are you hungry?"

She grins at me, and nods. "I didn't eat dinner yet."

"Did you have a plan for dinner, or can I take you out? I know a place in town with some great burgers and fries."

She laughs. "The Curly Pig it is then."

CHAPTER TWENTY

Gabby

The Curly Pig isn't my favorite place to be. It's usually too crowded for me. Tonight, with Heath by my side, it feels different—tolerable, at least. I watch as Heath takes a huge bite of his burger. "You've got a bit of mustard," I say, pointing to his chin.

"Thanks," he says, grabbing a napkin and wiping it off.

I'm glad we talked, but I can't help feeling a little raw still. Like a shirt tag rubbing on a sunburn. "Do you ever think things should be easier?" I ask. I always assumed love, when it was right, was easy. Heath and I feel right together, but it certainly has not been easy.

Heath shakes his head and swallows the bite he's just taken. "I've found that things that are worthwhile, the things that really matter, aren't always easy." He sits back in his chair and studies me. "Relationships are hard work, or so I've been told."

I nod. "I guess that makes sense." Gram always talked about Pops like he hung the moon. Maybe through the lens of her memories, their big problems seemed little after all.

I take one last look in the mirror before grabbing my boots and heading to the living room. Heath will be here any minute to pick me up for the Fall Festival. I slip my boots on and grab my purse just as there's a knock on the door.

"I'm ready," I say, swinging open the door.

Heath takes a step back and whistles. "My goodness, Gabby. You look gorgeous."

I fan the blush creeping up my neck. "It's just jeans and a t-shirt."

He shakes his head. "You could be in a potato sack, and you'd still be the most beautiful woman I've ever seen." He leans in and kisses my cheek. "Thank you for coming with me."

I step out onto the porch, closing the door behind me. "I'm excited." I lock the door and drop my keys into my purse. "I can't wait to see what Matti thinks of the festival."

Heath takes my hand and guides me to his truck. "I wonder if he'll want to ride any rides."

It doesn't take long to drive to the festival grounds and find parking. Knox, Lacey, and Matti are waiting for us at the entrance when we walk up. "About time you showed up," Lacey calls from the other side of the ticket stand. "Matti's ready to have some fun. Aren't you, buddy?"

Matti claps his hands from his seat in the stroller. "YES!" he squeals.

Heath pays for our tickets, laughing when Matti yells, "Let's go!"

"Where to first?" Knox asks, pushing the stroller forward.

"How about some of the smaller rides?" Lacey suggests. "The carousel was always a favorite of mine growing up."

We all agree, and make our way to the "Kidway," the section of rides and games geared towards little kids. After the carousel, where Matti picked a monkey, of all things, to ride, we head over to the bounce house.

"If you two will watch Matti, Heath and I will go grab us all some lemonade." Knox points to a food truck behind us.

"Only if you also get a funnel cake," Lacey says, grinning.

"You got it."

"So, how is everything going between you two?" Lacey asks.

"Things are going really great," I say. "Can I ask you something?"

She nods.

"Do you think love is supposed to be easy?"

Lacey laughs. "I wish. My mom and dad loved each other, and look how that turned out. Now they wish they had fought harder to be together back then. Life's all about choices. From what I can tell, choosing each other, even when it's hard, is what keeps love growing."

Lacey's grandparents had interfered and forced her parents apart when they were young. Now they're dating and Lacey's been shopping for formal dresses "just in case."

"Here we are," Knox says, walking up behind Lacey, a box filled with drinks and a funnel cake in his hands. "Did you miss me?"

Lacey smiles and takes her lemonade from his hand. "Always."

Heath hands me my cup and smiles. "Do you think he's ready to move on?" he says, gesturing to Matti who's literally bouncing off the walls of the bounce house.

Knox shakes his head. "I doubt it, he could be on this thing forever. Why don't you guys go ahead and we'll catch up with you in a bit."

"Are you sure?" We'd come together, and I knew we'd be spending most of our time following Matti around.

"Yes," Lacey says. "I've got a funnel cake to eat. Just save the tilt-a-whirl for me, you know it's our thing." She raises an eyebrow and points her finger at me. "No trying to get out of it either."

I groan. "You know that thing makes me want to throw up, right?"

Lacey cackles. "Yes, that's why I love it!"

"Let us know when you're ready to go to the petting zoo," Heath says. "It was always my favorite."

Knox and Lacey agree, and Heath takes my hand. "Well, where do you want to go now?"

"How about we see who can win a teddy bear?" I say, pointing to the water shooting race stand across the way.

Heath grins. "Remember the time I spent nearly a hundred dollars to win you that teddy bear you wanted?"

I nod. "I still have Mr. Fluffles, I'll have you know."

Heath leans in and plants a soft kiss right on my lips. "It was worth every penny."

Three rounds and thirty dollars later, we give up. "That was fun."

Heath laces his fingers through mine. "It was. Knox just texted they are headed to the petting zoo. Want to pet baby goats with me?"

"I thought you'd never ask." We walk hand in hand to the small enclosure that houses some goats, a chicken, a fluffy bunny, and a piglet. Matti is already inside feeding the goats from his hand.

"Hey," Knox says when we join them near the fence. "Now he wants a goat," he says, pointing to where Matti is now trying to hug the goats.

"Just tell him Flower would never allow it," I say. "Except she probably would. Flower is the most relaxed rescue dog I've ever seen."

Knox nods. "She'd probably want the goat to share her bed. Until he started trying to eat it, that is."

We all chuckle as Matti loses interest in hugging the goats and is crouched down near the bunny. "Maybe he needs a new pet," I suggest.

"No way," Lacey says, coming to stand near us and giving Matti room to roam on his own. "Flower is more than plenty. I think he's about tuckered out though."

"You two should go ride some rides before he's done," Heath says. "Knox and I will keep him entertained for a while longer."

"Thanks!" Lacey says, grabbing my hand and practically dragging me away toward the dreaded ride.

"I'll puke!" I protest. "I'm not kidding. I'm not eight years old anymore. I'll throw up."

She turns toward me and grins. "That's the fun part!"

Thankfully, I kept my food in my stomach . . . barely. "Let's head back to the guys," I say, trying to take deep breaths through my nose. "I don't think I can handle another ride right now."

Lacey laughs, but she looks a little green herself. "All right."

When we catch up with the guys, Matti is in the stroller rubbing his eyes. "I think it's time to go," Lacey says. "Thanks for spending a few hours with us."

"It was fun," I say, giving her a hug. "We'll have to do it again. Minus the tilt-a-whirl," I add.

"Want to ride the Ferris wheel?" Heath asks when we part ways. "I seem to remember the top being the best place to share a kiss."

Memories of that summer flood my mind. He'd driven me nearly two hours away to a small church fair, and we rode that Ferris wheel probably ten times just to share a kiss at the top. "I remember."

We wait in line, and Heath makes sure I get the inside seat when it's our turn to get on. Sitting side by side, my hand in his, as the cart slowly rises higher in the sky, my heart feels settled. "Almost at the top," I say softly, leaning against his shoulder.

He turns as we reach the top, causing me to sit up. Taking my face in his hands, he leans in and presses his lips against mine. The feeling of home, of love, of wholeness overcomes me.

"I love you," he whispers when he pulls back. "One day soon, I'm going to ask you to marry me like I should have done years ago."

I open my mouth to say something, but the words won't come.

"I just wanted to let you know," he says. "I know how you feel about surprises." He winks at me and pulls me in closer to his side.

"Do you really need all this candy?" Heath asks, looking at the three buckets I've got set up on a small table on the front porch.

"Absolutely. Big bars for the teenagers," I say, pointing. "Glow sticks and stuff for kids with food allergies. And snack-sized treats for everyone else."

Heath looks from one bucket to the next in awe. "You do this every Halloween?"

I nod. "It's a tradition I've kept going since Gram passed. Well, I added the blue bucket, but the rest is from her."

"I think the only Halloween tradition Mom and I had was getting a discount costume and walking the block." Heath smiles at me. "This is amazing."

A steady stream of superheroes, princesses, community helpers, and all kinds of other costumes I don't recognize quickly depletes the candy stash. "See," I say, as a group of teenagers walks away, a large chocolate bar in each of their hands. "This is why we have so much."

Heath looks inside the nearly empty buckets. "Maybe we should get more next year. I'd hate to run out."

My heart thumps against my ribs. Next year? "You want to do this again next year?"

He glances at me, and back to the cute little ballerina currently picking out a treat. "Of course. This year, and every year for the rest of our lives."

I step back, letting him man the table of candy. A vision of him in a few years, holding the hand of a little boy who looks just like him, while they walk around the neighborhood trick-or-treating steals my breath away. I slide down into the rocking chair that Gram used to call her thinking chair, and watch as he hands out candy, laughing with parents and patiently waiting for the kids to choose their favorites.

I want this, I realize. I want to create a family, pass out candy, go to the Fall Festivals and walk on the beach holding hands with him. Forever. Now, to show him I'm ready for that proposal.

CHAPTER TWENTY-ONE

Heath

After Halloween, it feels like something has changed in our relationship, but I can't figure out what. Things seem more comfortable—more steady. It's everything I've ever wanted. I just hope that feeling stays.

Knox and Lacey have invited us to see the Ozark Legends minor league game today. They are playing the Show Me State Space Cadets. Gabby and Lacey look adorable in their oversized jerseys.

"I hope we can keep up with what's going on," Lacey says to Gabby. "Knox and I have been watching baseball with Matti and I think I'm finally starting to understand."

Gabby grins. "I played softball growing up, remember?"

"That's right!" Lacey grins. "If I get confused, I'm asking you for help. It's embarrassing to ask your boyfriend sports questions."

Knox leans forward in his seat. "You know you can ask me anything."

Lacey grins, pops the hat off his head, and puts it on herself. "Oh, I know. Like, I *could* ask for your hat."

Knox pretends to be hurt, but winks at me over her head. Those two are sweet together. Just goes to show that sometimes opposites do attract.

Lacey dyed her hair a burnt kind of red for today's game since the Legends' colors are burgundy and gold. It seems like every time I see her, she's sporting a new hair color.

I reach over and run my fingers through Gabby's loose blonde hair. She turns and plants a kiss on my lips. "What was that for?" I ask.

"For being you," she says, before turning back to the game.

The score has been five to one since the bottom of the fourth inning. By the seventh inning stretch, the crowd has started thinning. "We're not leaving until the final out," Gabby says, flipping her hat upside down, the age-old tradition when your team is down. "Game's not over yet. Bases are loaded. Anything could happen!"

I laugh. *That's my girl.*

"How about Knox and I grab some hot dogs and popcorn for everyone?" I ask.

"Perfect," Lacey says, before jumping up when the umpire calls a strike.

Laughing, Knox and I make our way to the concessions area and wait in the line. We've just gotten our food when cheering erupts from the home crowd. We turn in time to see the batter cross home plate. "GRAND SLAM!" the announcer shouts. "Score is tied!"

We grab our food and hurry back to our seats. Gabby was right—game's not over yet!

The next two innings pass quickly. Both pitchers are doing their best to strike out the batters that step up to the plate. Finally, the Legends manage to get a huge hit to the outfield and win the scoring run.

Lacey and Gabby jump up and down in the aisle celebrating the win. "No wonder my brother-in-law loved baseball so much," Knox says to me. "That was exciting!"

"It was," I say, watching Gabby celebrate. "It really was."

The following Wednesday, Mom, Gabby and I are headed to Dominic and Olivia's for Thanksgiving. Mom was cleared to travel, and I've been missing Zade like crazy. I was hesitant to ask Gabby to join us. Not because I don't want her there, but because I know that Olivia is a sore spot for her.

"Ready to go?" I ask, putting the last of the bags into the trunk of Mom's car. We decided to take her car because we don't all fit in the truck, and as much as Gabby loves her Jeep, I'm not convinced it could make the eight-hour drive.

"Ready when you are," Gabby says from the front seat. Mom insisted she sit there, saying she needed the extra room in the back for her knitting supplies.

"All set," Mom calls.

"Let's get this show on the road," I say, shutting the trunk.

The drive is long. Mom spends time knitting and napping. Her two favorite things these days.

"What are you thinking?" I ask. Gabby's been singing along to the radio, but suddenly she's gone quiet.

"What if they don't like me?"

"Oh, Gabby." How could anyone not like her? "I promise, they'll love you."

"But what if they don't?" she asks, turning to face me. "Is that going to be a problem?"

I shake my head. "No. It won't be a problem. I love you, so they will love you." It's really that simple.

"Okay." Gabby turns to look out the window again.

"Gabby," I say softly, so I don't wake up Mom. "It's going to be okay." I had no idea she was nervous about them. Meanwhile, I'm nervous because, what if she doesn't like *them*? Olivia and Zade, and now Dominic, have been such a big part of my life these last few years.

"You're right," she says, placing her hand on my knee. The feeling of her warm palm on my jeans settles me, too.

"Hey," I say, gently shaking Gabby. "We're here."

She sits up, rubbing the sleep out of her eyes. "Already?"

I laugh. "You and Mom slept the last half of the trip."

"Sorry," she says, stretching. "I meant to stay awake and keep you company."

I lean in and kiss her cheek. She's too cute not to, all sleep-rumpled. "It's okay, I'm glad you were able to rest, because I can guarantee Zade will have you busy in no time."

She laughs and unbuckles her seatbelt. I get out and pop the trunk to get our stuff. Opening her door, she steps out of the car. Mom's already at the door with Zade in her arms. "I see someone is already in Grandma mode."

I hesitate, watching her face for any signs of distress.

As I drop the last bag at her feet, she turns to me and smiles. "It makes me wonder how she'll be when we have kids one day."

Just like that, my heart turns to a molten ball of gooey love and adoration for the woman standing in front of me. "She'll be like this, but worse," I say, smiling. I wish now that I'd brought the ring I've been storing in my nightstand since the weekend after the Fall Festival. I'd love nothing more than to drop to one knee and propose right here—in the driveway, with our luggage all around our feet. Okay, so maybe that's not the most romantic idea.

Olivia and Dominic step around the giggling duo on the front porch and come to help us with our bags. "It's good to meet you," Olivia says, pulling Gabby into a hug. "I feel like I've known you forever."

Gabby smiles. "It's good to finally meet you, too."

"Heath talked about you so much, I feel like we are already best friends." She grabs Gabby's hand and pulls her toward the house. "Come on. I'll give you a tour and we can gossip about our guys."

"Great idea." Gabby smiles at me as they walk off hand in hand.

"So," Dominic says. "Finally got the girl?"

I grin. "That's up to her."

He laughs. "Good man!"

After getting all the bags inside and into the guest room that Mom and Gabby will share, we head out to the backyard where Zade's convinced Mom to push him on the swing.

"We sure are glad you guys could make it," Olivia says. "I was worried, with your mom's health, you wouldn't be able to come."

I nod. "Me too."

"How is she?" Dominic asks, handing us each a cold bottle of water.

"She's good. Still weak and tired a lot, but much better than she was. The last set of scans was still clear, so the doctors are hopeful she's in remission."

Gabby leans in and takes my hand, immediately making the tension in my body release.

"I know it was hard on you not to be home with her. I was so glad when you took that weekend to visit her last Christmas," Olivia says, resting her head on Dominic's shoulder.

"You were home last Christmas?" Gabby asks. "I thought I saw you downtown, but you were gone before I could be sure."

Olivia chuckles. "He hid around the corner of the building when he spotted you."

I throw a pillow at her. "I didn't hide."

She laughs. "Okay, then what do you call it?"

"I realized I dropped something and needed to find it," I argue.

"Yeah—your *backbone*," Dominic says before bursting out in laughter.

Gabby squeezes my hand. "It's okay. I wouldn't have known what to say then, either."

I lean in and kiss her. "Thanks."

"Well, we'll let you guys get some rest," Olivia says. "Zade, time to get ready for bed."

"I'm not sleepy," Zade says, grabbing onto Mom's hand.

"I am, and I have to share a room with you tonight, remember? You better go get ready like your mom asked so I can read you a bedtime story before I fall asleep." I yawn and stretch like I'm ready for bed. "I'm so tired, I could fall asleep any minute."

"Wait for me!" Zade calls, running into the house.

Dominic laughs. "I swear he'd do anything you say."

I shrug. "Probably because I don't see him as much these days."

Mom giggles and shakes her head. "Kids always listen to others better than their parents. He's a good kid."

Dominic nods. "That he is." He shares a look with Olivia who shakes her head slightly.

"Okay . . ." I say, confused by whatever that was. "What's going on? Is something wrong with Zade?"

"No, nothing like that," Olivia says. "We have some news, but we are waiting until tomorrow when everyone is here to share."

I raise an eyebrow. "Good news?"

Olivia nods and Dominic pulls her close. "Great news."

I nod. "Okay, then, I can wait."

Gabby gasps. "You can wait? *I* can't wait!" She giggles. "I hate surprises."

Olivia laughs. "Noted. Help yourselves to anything you need," she says, yawning for real. "I'm exhausted. See you in the morning."

After a round of goodnights, everyone splits off to their rooms. Zade is sitting up in his twin bed, his animal sheets spread across his lap, and a book on zoo animals laid out in front of him.

"Can you read me this one?" he says, picking up the book and handing it to me.

"You got it," I say, ruffling his hair. I'm three pages in when I hear him snoring softly. I lay the book down and settle into the air mattress on the floor. I wonder how it will feel to read bedtime stories to my own kids one day. Zade rolls over and sighs.

If it feels anything like this, I can't wait.

Chapter Twenty-Two

Gabby

I'd thought coming to Kentucky and meeting Olivia and her family would be hard, but from the moment we met, she's been nothing less than amazing. I can see how she and Heath quickly became friends. Watching them together this evening, it was clear they love each other like siblings. I'm glad he had that kind of support while he was gone, serving his country away from his mom and the only people he'd ever known.

I feel a bit guilty about how jealous I've been. I have to let that go. It's obvious Olivia and Zade mean a lot to Heath, and that he means a lot to them. There's no way I'd want to step in and mess that up. They are his family, too.

Family.

Olivia and Dominic move together with ease, but I know from what Heath has shared with me, it hasn't always been this way. They've had their ups and downs, too. Lacey was right—love is about choosing each other when the hard times come.

Can I see myself choosing Heath time and time again? Yes. There's no doubt in my mind. I'd choose him a million times if it meant loving him for the rest of my life.

I wake to the smell of turkey roasting in the oven. Opening my eyes, I roll over and see Rosie is already up and out of the room. What time is it?

I reach for my phone on the nightstand, squinting when the bright light hits my eyes. Eleven o'clock. Shoot!

I jump out of the bed and rummage through my suitcase for my clothes. How did I sleep so late?

Finally dressed for the day, I follow the scent of delicious food and coffee back to the kitchen. I hear Heath and Olivia's voices as I come down the hall and pause.

"Are you sure she's ready for this?" I hear Olivia ask.

"I think so," Heath says. "I'm ready."

Olivia chuckles. "Yeah, but just because you're ready doesn't mean you're on the same page. You have to communicate."

I can hear him mumble something, but I don't want to be caught eavesdropping. "What is that delicious smell?" I ask loudly as I step into the kitchen.

Olivia points to the counter. "We left you some breakfast options out, and there's coffee in the pot. Cups are in the cabinet right above."

"Thanks," I say, grabbing a plate and filling it with fruit and a muffin. "Sorry I slept so late. Do you need help with anything?"

Heath hands me a cup of coffee and smiles. "I'm helping, you sit and eat, sleepyhead." He kisses my forehead and motions toward the table.

I take a bite of muffin and groan.

"Someone was hungry," I hear Olivia say, just before the doorbell rings. "That must be my parents. Heath, can you get the door?"

"Where is everyone else?" I ask between bites.

"Dominic, Rosie, and Zade are on a walk. Zade wanted to show Rosie how he can ride his bike now."

"That's sweet. I love how close the two of them are." I stand and take my empty plate to the sink.

"Heath and his mom have been a godsend. I didn't know what I was going to do when I found out I was pregnant. They stepped up and were by my side through it all."

I nod. "They are really wonderful people; I'd expect nothing less."

Olivia grimaces. "I'm just sorry you were hurt in the process."

"Oh, you're sweet. I wasn't in a good place back then, but that was a long time ago."

"For what it's worth," Olivia says. "Heath was devastated."

I glance down the hall where Heath is approaching with an older couple. "I know."

"Olivia, dear," a well-dressed woman says. She has the neatest bob I've ever seen. "So glad we could make it."

"Hi, Mom. Hi, Dad." Olivia hugs them each in turn. "I'm glad you could come this year, too."

"Where is our grandson?" her dad asks, looking around.

"He's on a bike ride with Dom and his Grandma Rosie." Olivia ignores the pinched expression on her mom's face. "They should be back any minute. Let me introduce you."

She motions toward me. "This is Gabby, Heath's girlfriend. You know Heath. Gabby, this is my mom, Loryn and my dad, Alfredo."

"Nice to meet you," I say, holding my hand out to each of them. "You've raised a wonderful daughter."

"Thank you," Loryn says. "Olivia, what time will we be eating?"

"In an hour or so," she says, checking the thermometer readout near the oven. "The turkey's almost done."

"Oh good," her mom says. "We have drinks this evening with the Lamberts."

The sound of the front door swinging open and the clomp of little running feet pull everyone's attention from the food.

"Grandma, Grandpa, you're here!" Zade comes to a stop just in front of his grandparents and waits for them to hug him.

"Nice to see you, Zade," Alfredo says, patting him on the back.

"Want to see my tree house?" Zade asks.

"Come on," Dominic says, leading the way to the back door. "I'll get you set up on the porch and you can watch him play."

Once everyone is outside, Olivia sags. "Every time," she mutters.

"You okay?" I ask.

"Yeah. I don't know why I was hoping they'd be less stiff with Zade once he was older. They haven't ever been very affectionate people."

"I'm sorry," I say, thinking of my own mom. She was great when I was little, but as soon as she met her now-husband, I was left behind.

"It's okay." She turns and busies herself with the mashed potatoes.

Olivia is pulling the turkey from the oven when the doorbell rings again. "I'll get it," Dominic says, coming through the back door.

We hear him greet the newcomers and he leads them into the kitchen.

"My parents, Debbie and Marco," he says, touching each of them on the shoulder. "This is Gabby, Heath's girlfriend." They smile and shake hands with everyone, then step outside and get tackled by Zade.

Once the greetings are over, Dominic ushers everyone into the dining room where the table is set and decorated to the nines and place cards have been set out. It's beautiful. So beautiful I don't want to sit down and mess it up.

"You're by me," Heath says, pulling out the seat between him and his mom.

Dominic and Olivia finish bringing the dishes to the table, and Dominic says the prayer. "Who's ready to eat?" he asks.

"I am!" Zade's hand shoots up into the air.

Everyone chuckles and before long, plates are filled and conversation starts flowing. It's not as comfortable as being at Mrs. Chambers's house, but I've known her most of my life, so that's no surprise.

A tinkling of silverware on glass causes the conversation to stop abruptly. Standing, Dominic helps Olivia to her feet and pulls her close. Heath reaches for my hand under the table.

"Thank you all for joining us today. We're thrilled our families could be here with us for Thanksgiving. Speaking of being thankful, we'd like to share some news." He takes his time, looking at each of us. Zade is wiggling in his seat, still happily shoveling mashed potatoes and corn into his mouth.

"As you know, Olivia has decided to retire from the Army. Her contract will be up at the end of January."

"About time," her dad says, not so quietly.

Olivia looks like she might cry. I can understand why she's found so much comfort in having Rosie as a surrogate mother and grandmother.

"Yes, well, that's not the only news." He pulls Olivia to him, planting a kiss on the top of her head. "We are expanding our family. Olivia is pregnant!"

To say the reaction was mixed would be an understatement. Her parents pushed back from the table, gathered their things and left without a word.

Dominic's parents, on the other hand, were overjoyed at the thought of another little one to spoil, and when Rosie found out she'd be an honorary grandma again, she beamed like the North Star.

"Congratulations," Heath says, hugging first Olivia and then Dominic. "I'm so excited to be an uncle again!"

"Who knows," Dominic says. "Maybe your kids can play with our kids before too long."

Heath looks at me and smiles. "Maybe."

The rest of the afternoon is spent in easy conversation. Dominic's parents get down on the floor and play dinosaurs with Zade, making everyone laugh. Heath is Zade's personal jungle gym for a while, soaking up every last moment of time before we need to leave.

Unfortunately, that time comes sooner than anyone is ready for.

"Thank you for coming," Olivia says, pulling me in for a hug. "I'll be calling you and keeping tabs on this one." She points to Heath and grins. "If he does anything stupid, you call me."

I laugh. "I'm sure I won't need to. He's pretty perfect."

"So does this mean we'll be seeing more of you?" Dominic asks, walking us out to the car.

"Absolutely," Heath says, wrapping his arms around me.

"Good," Dominic says.

"Come on, Mom," Heath calls. "We need to get going."

"Aww," Rosie and Zade call at the same time.

Pulling out of the driveway, it truly feels like leaving a bit of family behind. "Think they'd ever move to Piney Brook?" I ask.

"I already asked," Rosie says from the back seat. "It wasn't a no."

Heath laughs. "That would require Dominic leaving the Army, but you never know. He should be up for retirement soon."

For the first time in a long time, I feel like I have family. I glance across the car at Heath and smile. I think back to the years I was wrong about him because I was too hurt to see the truth. He broke up with me back then because he thought it was best for *me*. He helped Olivia because he cared more for her situation than he did for his own reputation. He consistently makes choices for the good of others, disregarding his own wishes. This is the man I want to marry.

I wouldn't change the past if I could. It's made us stronger. It's crystal clear now—I want forever with this man. A man who does the right thing, even when it causes him pain.

My first love.

My one and only.

Chapter Twenty-Three

Heath

"Hey, boss," I call, walking into the old bank building we just started renovating to turn it into a veterinarian's office and a groomer. "How was your Thanksgiving?"

Bradley sets down the clipboard he was looking at and smiles. "It was pretty good. How was your holiday? You guys left, right?"

I nod. "We did. We drove to Kentucky to visit family."

"I heard a special someone may have gone with you." He raises an eyebrow. "Have you two finally figured it all out?"

I laugh. "I don't know about having it all figured out, but we are in a good place. So good, in fact, I'm planning to propose soon."

Hudson chooses that moment to come around the corner, Parker trailing close behind him. "Propose! You're going to make me the only single guy on the crew? Not cool, man. Not cool."

"Hudson, if I waited for you to settle down, I'd be old and gray."

He laughs. "Sounds about right. I don't see why everyone wants to settle down so bad."

Parkers's phone rings. He holds it up and motions outside. "My wife," he says, stepping out the doors.

"See what I mean?" Hudson says, shaking his head. "No thanks. I don't want to answer to anyone else."

I chuckle. "I've known what I wanted since I was eighteen. Younger, even, but at first I was too scared to admit I'd fallen for my best friend."

He throws his hands out in front of him. "Keep those love germs over there. I hear they're contagious."

Laughing, I put my hard hat on and check the clipboard for what I'm working on today.

Thankfully, the day passes quickly, and I'm ready to leave right at five o'clock. "See you guys tomorrow," I call to the crew.

Once I'm in the truck, I pull out my phone.

Heath: I miss you.

I put the phone in the seat next to me and head home to shower. The phone dings with an incoming text as I'm drying my hair. I grab the phone and smile when I see it's from Gabby.

Gabby: I miss you, too. Feel like company?

I do a little dance and head to the dresser to pick out something comfortable to wear before texting her back.

Heath: Of course. Come on over. I'll order some pizza.

Thirty minutes later, there's a knock at the door, and I'm letting the love of my life into the house. "I'm so glad you came over," I say, stepping into her space and kissing her cheek.

"Me, too." She slips out of her shoes and heads to the living room. "Where's Momma A?"

"She's with her support group tonight," I say, following her. "Pizza should be here soon."

We sit down on the couch, and she reaches for my hands.

A feeling of dread pools in my stomach as I study her eyes. "Everything okay?" She's acting weird, and it's scaring me a little.

She nods. "I think we should talk."

Nothing good ever comes from those five words.

"Okay," I say. Settling back into the couch. "What would you like to talk about?"

"You are the best man I know, Heath. I've been thinking about how wrong I was to shut you out for so long. I'm so sorry."

"We can't change the past, remember?"

"I know." She takes a deep breath and lets it out slowly. "Did you mean it?"

"Mean what?" I'm so confused.

She shakes her head. "Did you mean it when you told me you were going to propose soon?"

I nod. "I did."

She stands up and drops to one knee. "What if I do it first?"

I leap off the couch and lift her off the floor. "Go put your shoes on," I say, kissing her lips and sprinting down the hallway to my room.

There's no way I'm letting her propose first. I planned this, and I'm going to do it. I send a text and cross my fingers that it reaches its target in time.

When I meet her in the front hallway, she's got her shoes on and an uncertain look on her face. "I promise, it's all going to be okay. Just go for a ride with me?"

She nods.

I help her into my truck and close her door. I walk around to my side and get in, starting the truck and taking a deep breath. This is the last time I'm leaving my house as a boyfriend, unless I really mess this up.

"Wait!" Gabby says, causing me to step on the brake. "What about the pizza?"

I grab my phone and call the pizza place, and get the same kid who took my order earlier.

"Hey, Dale. I had a . . . meeting come up, and had to leave home, so you and the driver can keep my order for yourselves tonight, okay? Thanks."

I reach for Gabby's hand and squeeze. "I'll make sure we eat something soon, okay?"

Gabby nods. "Okay."

With that settled, I drive to the high school, and pull up just outside the gym where our prom was held.

"What are we doing here?" Gabby asks, looking around. "You know the school's closed, right?"

I nod. "I do. Just trust me okay?"

I help her out of the truck and walk with her to the entrance of the gymnasium. Grabbing the door, I pray that Old Mr. Janowitz got my message. I pull on the handle, and the door creaks open. The emergency lights provide the only spots of light in the space.

"How did you . . . ?" Gabby asks, before she turns to look at me.

I sink to one knee and hold out the ring box I've been keeping in my pocket. "Gabby, this room is where I realized how beautiful you were. It's where I held you close, and we slow-danced to Ed Sheeran's "Perfect." It's where I started wishing that one day you'd be mine. So, I wanted to come back here and make that wish come true." I take a breath and open the ring box. "Gabrielle Louise Fineman, will you do me the honor of becoming my wife?"

She stands there, her hair in a messy bun, tears sliding down her face, and all I can think is how much more beautiful she is tonight than she was that night all those years ago. "Please?" I say when she doesn't answer me.

"Yes!" she shouts, putting out her hand for me to slip the ring on her finger. "Yes, of course I'll marry you."

She leaps into my arms, and I kiss her like my life depends on it. Every ounce of emotion, love, happiness, relief—I let it flow through that kiss.

A slow clap breaks us apart as Mr. Janowitz comes to join us in the center of the room. "I'm happy for you two," he says, a smile on his face. "Mrs. G and I figured it would happen sooner or later."

"You and Mrs. G?" Gabby asks.

He nods. "We've been watching you two since you were in high school. I bet you'd be together by the time he left for the Army, but I lost that bet."

Heath grins. "Not really. We were together then. We were just too young to know how to handle such a big relationship long distance."

"Well, I'll be," Mr. Janowitz says. "I'll be getting my winnings from Gertie, then."

"Thank you for opening the gymnasium," I say. "Especially on short notice."

"You're welcome. Anything for true love."

I kiss Gabby again. "Ready to go spread the news?"

She laughs. "What?"

"I called my mom when I went to my room to get the ring." I shrug. "I'm sure she's assembled everyone by now."

Gabby grins. "Then I guess it's time we let everyone know I'm going to be Mrs. Gabrielle Atkins."

I call Mom and smile, mouthing "I told you" as she's talking. "We're on our way," I say, ending the call.

I open the truck door and help Gabby inside. "So, when do you want to get married?" I ask. "I vote sooner rather than later."

She laughs. "We just got engaged, and you already want to be married?"

I close her door and run around to my side. Hopping up, I look at her and grin. "I've spent enough time not married to you."

She sits back, admiring the princess-cut diamond set in white gold I placed on her finger. "I want our family to be there," she says.

"Whoever you want," I agree.

"Nothing big?" she asks.

I shake my head. "Close friends and family sounds good to me."

"Then let's get married this spring when Zade has spring break."

"Perfect," I say, grabbing my phone. "Let's make sure they don't make plans." I dial the phone and put it on speaker. Olivia picks up on the first ring. "I'm getting married during spring break. When is spring break?"

She laughs. "I'm so happy for you two," she shouts. "Zade! Dominic! Heath and Gabby are getting married!"

I wait for everyone to calm down and repeat my question. "When is Zade's spring break? Gabby insists we wait until our family can all be together, and I don't want to wait a minute longer to become her husband."

"I like her," Olivia says. "His spring break is in March. Think you can pull a wedding together in three months?"

I look at Gabby and grin. "I'd do anything for her."

Epilogue

The following year

I'm walking out of the florist's office when my phone rings. I laugh when I see Evan's name pop up on my screen. Man, he's nervous! "Hey, I'm ready," I say in greeting.

He laughs. "I didn't even ask you yet."

"I know, but you've been stressing about the details for days. I'm on my way to pick up the flowers now. It's all a go." I thought I was nervous about getting married. Evan's a mess, and he's just popping the question!

"Thanks, man. I appreciate your help."

I laugh out loud. "Like I'd let you do this alone." He was there beside me on my wedding day, and I'll do the same for him. Growing up, Evan was like a brother to me. Now that we are adults, that sense of found family is even stronger.

"I'll be waiting," I say, and hang up.

I switch to Gabby's number and hit dial. "Hey, darlin'," I say when she answers. "You guys doing okay?" I left her home alone with Olivia, Scarlette and Zade. Dominic hasn't been able to take leave, but since Olivia retired from the Army, she decided to homeschool Zade. Which meant they could come and join us for the Fall Festival this year.

"We're getting ready now. We'll meet you there?"

Gabby's sweet voice never fails to put a smile on my face. "I can't wait."

Hanging up the phone, I click the button to unlock the fancy new SUV we purchased last week. Sliding inside, I place the flowers in the passenger seat, and look to the rear, imagining what a car seat will look like buckled into the middle of the back row.

I pull into the parking lot of the festival with plenty of time to spare. Grabbing the flowers, I hop out and hit the lock button. I grab a ticket and make my way past the games to the rear of the festivities. I pick a bench near the Ferris wheel, and wait for them to show up.

"Hey, Heath's here too," Karlee says as they get closer.

I pretend not to notice them walking up, making sure the bouquet is well hidden.

"Heath!" Karlee calls.

I look in their direction and wave, one hand hidden behind my back. "Oh, hey," I say, smiling at her. "I didn't expect to see you here."

Evan grins and gives me a thumbs up behind her back.

"It was going to be a girls' day, but the guys found a sitter and decided to join us." She points over her shoulder. "What are you doing here?"

"Oh," I say. Panicking a bit. Evan and I hadn't talked about why I would be here alone. "I was hoping to bump into this girl I know," I say, my lame attempt at a joke falling flat.

"Oh, have you found her?" Karlee asks, looking around for Gabby.

"No, not yet. I'm sure I'll run into her, though. She was meeting me here." At least that part's true.

She nods. "Well, you're welcome to join us until she shows up."

"Nah, I'm going to keep moving and see if I can find her. Thanks, though."

"Better get in line," Evan says, guiding her to the end of the line.

I wait until she's distracted, cross behind them, and pass the flowers to Evan without her seeing. Phew, Operation Evan Proposes is in play. I can't contain my smile as they get in the passenger pod and Evan passes her the flowers. Her stunned expression makes every moment of today worth it. I'm so happy for them. If they can find half as much joy in marriage as Gabby and I have, they will be happy the rest of their days.

I watch as they make it to the top and Evan pulls out the ring. When she says yes, the crowd around the ride claps and congratulates them loudly.

I glance at my watch. Gabby and Olivia should be here with the kids now. We invited Mom, but she didn't feel up to being out at the fair today. Truth be told, I think she was looking forward to seeing her newest friend from the cancer support group. Jim has been coming over nearly every day. Mom thinks I don't know just because I got married and moved out.

As if I don't drive by and check in on Mom every day. After interrupting their dinner twice, I now know to keep driving when I see his car parked out front, and then I call her instead.

It's worked so far, but eventually, she's going to have to tell me about her special friend.

"There you are!" Gabby says when I meet up with them near the entrance. "How'd it go?"

I grin. "She said yes," I say, chuckling. "He managed to pull it off."

"Yay!" Gabby does a happy dance. "I'm so happy for them."

I pull her close, placing my hand on her stomach. "I am too," I say before giving her a kiss.

"Eww," Zade says, covering his eyes with his hands. "Why do grown-ups kiss so much?"

I laugh. "You'll understand one day. When you find the person your soul doesn't want to live without."

He shakes his head. "Nuh-uh, that's gross."

Olivia laughs. "Keep thinking that."

We spend the afternoon taking Zade on all the rides and stopping at several of the game booths before calling it quits and heading back home for dinner.

"Mom's here," I call from my spot on the couch, baby Scarlette nestled in my arms. I can't wait to hold my own baby soon.

"Grandma!" Zade yells, running to the front door. "Can I open it?"

"Yes," Olivia calls from the kitchen. "Just be careful not to knock her over."

Mom's scans have been clean, and she's getting stronger, but she's still more fragile than she was before. Hopefully the cancer doesn't come back, but if it does, we'll be ready to support her.

Zade flings open the door and stops short. "Grandma has a friend," he calls.

"I hope you don't mind," Mom says, stepping into the house. "I invited Jim." She blushes—a phenomenon I'm not sure I've ever seen on her.

"Of course we don't mind," Olivia says, wiping her hands on a towel and greeting them. "Nice to meet you, Jim. Any friend of Rosie's is always welcome."

Once the introductions are made, I pass the baby back to Olivia and help Gabby take the dishes into the dining room and set the table. "Are you ready?" I ask her, giving her a kiss on my way past her to the kitchen to grab the rest of the food.

She nods and rubs her hand over her stomach nervously. "I think so."

It had been a rough first trimester. Between spotting, nausea and the extreme fatigue, it had been all I could do to convince her to take fewer shifts on the floor. Thankfully, managing the diner gave her plenty of opportunities to work and sit at the same time.

Now that she's in the second trimester, she's been feeling a lot better and is ready to share our news.

"Dinner's ready," I call out. Mom, Jim, Olivia with the baby, and Zade all make their way into the dining room and squeeze around the table.

"Here," Gabby says. "I'll take her and lay her down in the playpen if you want."

"Thanks," Olivia says, gently passing the baby to Gabby. "Let's hope she sleeps long enough for me to eat."

Gabby disappears down the hallway with the baby. A few minutes later, she returns with the baby monitor and sets it on the table by Olivia. "She's out cold."

"I have an announcement of sorts," Mom says once everyone has their plates made. "Jim and I are dating." He reaches over and takes her hand.

"Your mother is a very special woman," Jim says, looking at me.

"I know," I say, holding eye contact. "Be good to her, and I'll be happy."

He nods. "That's my plan." He lets go of her hand and picks up his fork to eat.

"Well then," Olivia says, grinning. "If we're making announcements, I have one, too."

I groan. *Seriously?*

"What?" she asks.

"I'm hungry," I say, deflecting.

"You can wait another minute. Dominic is retiring, and we are moving to Piney Brook!" Zade claps his hands. "We'll be close enough to see you every day, Grandma!"

Mom chuckles. "I can't wait!"

I glance at Gabby and shrug. May as well.

"Before we actually get to eating, I guess it's our turn." I stand and move behind Gabby. Placing my hand on her shoulder, I give it a squeeze for support.

"I'm four-months pregnant," Gabby says.

Everyone cheers and congratulates us.

"Looks like we'll be close enough to babysit for each other," Olivia says.

"I was hoping you'd say that," Gabby says. "I was going to ask you to watch the baby when I go back to work."

I sit back down at the head of the table and half listen to the chatter around me. Mom's healthy, and she's found someone that makes her happy. Olivia and Dominic are moving to town with Zade and Scarlette, and the love of my life is having my baby. It doesn't get any better than this.

If you enjoyed Heath and Gabby's story, I'd love for you to leave a review. Even a star rating helps authors get seen.

Want to know why Aurora is so aggravated by Bradley? Check out their story in You Mocha Me Crazy.

About the Author

Tia Marlee resides in Central Texas with her husband and three teenaged children. When she isn't writing, Tia enjoys reading, embroidery and spending time with her family. Tia is the author of the Piney Book Wishes series featuring unexpected love stories based in small-town Piney Brook, Arkansas. Tia is thrilled to have joined the fun, romantic comedy series The Coffee Loft with several of her sweet author friends. Set in the same small town, Tia has connected these deliciously warm romcoms to her Piney Brook Wishes series.

Let's Stay In Touch

You can find me at my website: https://tiamarlee.com
Follow me:
Facebook: https://tinyurl.com/FBTiaMarlee
Instagram: https://tinyurl.com/IGTiaMarlee
Amazon: https://tinyurl.com/AmazonTiaMarlee
BookBub: https://tinyurl.com/BBTiaMarlee
Goodreads: https://tinyurl.com/GRTiaMarlee

Join my reader group: https://tinyurl.com/TiaMarleeReaderGroup

Also By Tia Marlee

Piney Brook Wishes Series
His Christmas Wish
Sweet Summertime Wishes
Wishing for the Girl Next Door
A Soldier's Wish

The Coffee Loft Series
Bean Wishing for a Latte Love
You Mocha Me Crazy

Printed in Great Britain
by Amazon